RIDING FOR REVENGE

"Sheriff, tell me about those three men," Spur said.

"Whatever they done is my responsibility," Sloan said. "Wish I could charge them with murder, but that would be hard to do, you walking around and all. I can charge them with *attempted* murder, but our judges don't hold much with that kind of legal maneuvering."

"They think they killed me," Spur said slowly. "I just might be able to scare them to death. Tell me about them."

"Thought you had an assignment here?"

"Do, but it can wait a day or two. Tell me."

"Boots Dallman is the blond guy. Surprised he went along with it, but then figured out he was still drunk. Gabe Young had him scared to death out there."

"I had the same feeling," Spur said. "What about Young?"

"Been in trouble in half of the state. Drifter, gambler, gun for hire sometimes. A killer who doesn't care who goes down. Other man is Joshua Hoffer, a merchant in town but not exactly a lily-white character."

"Bloodthirsty little bastard," Spur said, the croak coming back into his voice. "Way I look at it, if one or two of these guys has an accident it would be mighty hard to prove it was murder."

"McCoy, you had a rough time, but you're alive. It's better than being dead. I helped keep you alive. Don't make me move against you."

"Sheriff, you ever been hanged?"

The big man on the black horse shook his head slowly.

"Then don't be telling me what I can and can't do, not until you've walked at least a mile in the boots of a man who has been!"

SPUR #15

HANG SPUR McCOY!

DIRK FLETCHER

LEISURE BOOKS NEW YORK CITY

A LEISURE BOOK®

August 2004

Published by

Dorchester Publishing Co., Inc.
200 Madison Avenue
New York, NY 10016

ISBN 0-8439-2346-6

The name "Leisure Books" and the stylized "L" with design are
trademarks of Dorchester Publishing Co., Inc.

Printed in the United States of America.

Visit us on the web at www.dorchesterpub.com.

SPUR #15

HANG SPUR McCOY!

1

A rifle slug smashed into the boulder Spur McCoy huddled behind, hitting only six inches above his head, shattering the lead and tearing sharp granite shards off the rock and spewing them behind him. The shot came so close McCoy could smell the burned black powder. He jerked his head down at once and moved to the far side of the horse-sized upthrust of natural rock protection.

Spur leaned out and fired the Spencer repeating rifle as quickly as he could, levering the second round in, only half aiming as he sent the thundering .52 caliber chunks of hot lead toward the outhouse thirty yards to the rear of the small ranch cabin a hundred yards below him in the farthest end of the small valley.

Spur McCoy was a big man with sandy brown hair, a full brown mustache and mutton chop sideburns. He was one of the few United States Secret Service Agents in the West and roamed half the nation on assignments straight from Washing-

7

ton, D.C. usually via the telegraph key. But this was
one job he had stumbled into on his own.

The man Spur had shot at behind the facility
decided he'd been exposed too much and for too
long. He ran for the house, firing a shot from his rifle
toward Spur as he ran. Spur leavered around the
rock, aimed, followed, then led the runner and fired.
It was like gunning a duck on the wing or at a
bouncing mule deer running across your path.

The lead was exactly right. The .52 caliber slug
bored through the left side of the gunman, churned
through muscle, tissue and small bones, smashing a
rib and continuing in six pieces straight into the
gunman's heart. The attacker stumbled and fell, his
rifle skittering ahead of him, his hands thrown out
in fatal protest. His chest hit in the reddish brown
dirt first, then his head flopped forward and his face
gouged a two foot trail in the dust before his body
came to a stop.

As soon as he saw the hit, Spur turned his sights
on the small cabin. It was typical of the kind of
domiciles homesteaders threw up to meet the terms
of *improving* the land. That meant first a house, and
then a barn or corral, and of course a herd of steers
or milk cows, or some evidence that tilling the soil
had been undertaken. Here in this southern Idaho
valley not far south of the Snake river, it was cattle.

Spur was berating himself for getting caught in
such an awkward situation in the first place. He had
been on his way to Twin Falls, Idaho, in the
southern part of the state, after coming most of the
way from Pocatello on the stage. At a stage over-
night stop he had been told of massive Indian
gatherings ten miles to the north. He fought the
idea, but at last his conscience won. He was
probably the only federal lawman within a thousand

miles, and if there was a large number of Indians grouping for some kind of attack . . .

He had rented a horse and investigated, then discovered only a family meeting of fifteen Shoshoni Indians from the same tribe. They were branches of the same family and had been separated for almost a year. It was a reunion. They were so friendly and peaceful, that it took Spur two days to pay his respects and get back on his way toward Twin Falls.

The "massive" gathering of Shoshoni had congregated to harvest a particularly tasty variety of wild onions, which they harvested and dried for use later in the winter. They also gathered acorns and pine nuts for their winter lodges. The Shoshoni were just as well known as "the grass people," since they were not hunters or agricultural, but roamed wherever they might find food and buffalo.

Another bullet whined away from the rock Spur lay behind. He moved to the other side and peered over a mound of decomposing granite.

A small yard in front of the house held a well, a hitching post and the sprawled body of a man Spur guessed was the owner of the homestead. Spur had seen two men charge into the house and heard shots, but now all was quiet.

A horse whickered from behind the house. He heard leather creaking in the silent mountain air.

They were moving out!

Spur jumped up and ran downhill until he could see around the side of the cabin. The third man swung up on his horse. Spur jerked up the Spencer and sent two rounds at them, but the quickly aimed shots missed. He saw puffs of smoke where the rifles below him returned fire.

Something hit him hard in the right leg. His last shot went into the air as he spun backward and tumbled into the dirt. The pain came in gushing waves as he looked down at his leg. Already his pants leg was red with blood. He lay down the Spencer and watched the three horsemen charge away from him, bent low in the saddle to make the smallest targets possible.

McCoy felt sweat pop out on his forehead. The waves of pain plowed through him as he tried to sit up. He made it only by pushing with his right hand. His whole lower pants leg was red-wet with blood.

He had to stop the flow. He pulled his knife and slit the pants leg from the knee down. The ugly gash pulsed blood out of his leg with every heartbeat. Spur pulled off his neckerchief and wrapped it around the wound, then tugged the cloth as tight as he could.

A vicious, thundering hammering slammed into his head, then everything faded into gray and splotches of black as the knife edges of pain sliced patterns through his brain. He blinked and shook his head until it cleared. He had seldom felt pain so pervasive.

How could he lose so much blood so fast? His vision returned to near normal. There was no possibility that he could get to the well for water, not unless he hopped, or dragged his wounded right leg. But he had to try or he would die where he lay. He tucked the ends of the kerchief under the last wrapping and decided the makeshift bandage would stay in place. He had to get moving. If he stayed there he would be some hungry buzzard's breakfast.

McCoy gritted his teeth, picked up the Spencer and slid forward a foot toward the well. He pushed with his left foot, letting his right leg drag. Sweat ran into his eyes. The sun beamed down in all its noontime splendor and heat.

Ten minutes later he had moved thirty feet. Behind him he could see where his leg made a trail in the red shot soil. Here and there were splotches of blood.

His eyes clouded again, and this time it took him longer to clear his vision. Another half hour and he would be in the shade of the little well house.

If he made it.

How had he lost so much blood so quickly? The bullet must have hit an artery.

For a moment he thought he heard hoofbeats through the ground. He put both hands flat on the ground and listened. A bird called somewhere in the woods a quarter of a mile north. Then he felt the vibrations, horses were coming.

Quickly he picked up the Spencer and levered a fresh round in. If the killers were coming back, he should be able to get one more of them before they finished him. Two for one, not too bad.

The shapes on horseback wavered through the heat at first. They did not seem to be attacking. Four of them at least, he decided. Another cloud covered his eyes and he had to rub them to bring back the light.

At last he spotted the riders again, four, riding fast. They had guns out now, but no one was shooting. As they came closer he thought he noticed something on one man's shirt. Then he saw it again. The sun glinted off a silver star. Yes, a marshall or a sheriff. Good, he might just make it yet.

Then the cloud closed in around him, the sky darkened, and Spur McCoy fell forward his head resting on his arm, as unconsciousness overwhelmed him.

Cold.

Something cold.

He felt it again. This time it came suddenly and he snorted, gasped and his eyes jolted open. His face was wet. Someone had thrown water in his face. He tried to sit up.

Hands held him down. He was out of the sun. Spur frowned, then looked up at the closest face. His vision was clear. He saw the badge on a slightly out of focus chest, then a full moustache on a stubble-cheeked face with large brown eyes that were now bloodshot and weary.

"Come on, damnit! You've had enough sleep." The sheriff slapped Spur's cheeks gently. "Wake up, man. We've got the blood stopped. I want to know who the hell you are."

Spur saw it was the man with the badge talking. He faded out of focus, then came back sharp and clear. Spur frowned and blinked.

"Drink?" Spur asked, his voice low, uncertain.

The same big man held Spur's shoulders and gave him water from a tin cup. With the water Spur gained strength and sat up. Three other men were in the fuzzy background on the cabin's rough porch.

Spur saw the word "Sheriff" on the silver badge.

"Name is Spur McCoy, Sheriff. Going to Twin Falls on business."

"Or you just come from there," a nasty voice said from the shadows. Spur could not see the man who spoke.

"Give him his say," the sheriff snapped. He looked at Spur. "I'm Sheriff Sloan of Twin Falls County. I'm the law here."

"Howdy. I was south into the mountains a ways and coming back toward the stage road when I heard some shots. When I got over here I saw these four guys had surrounded the cabin and were shooting up a small war. One man was already dead out by the well."

"You was one of the killers, wasn't you, asshole?" The slurred, angry words came from a man who leaned down into Spur's face. He had thin features and wore an expression of abject hatred. His small, tight mouth never smiled.

"No, I wasn't with them," Spur said. "I was fighting them."

"He's about the right size," a new, older voice said from behind Spur. "Horse is the right color, and his hat even matches. We found his Spencer 7-shot rifle, too. Hell, that's more than enough for me."

Sheriff Sloan sat back on his heels. "Get this straight, you three. This is a duly constituted posse, not a damn lynch party. You're working under me. You will take all of your orders from me. Any disagreement with my orders and you're in your saddle heading back to town. I'll do the questioning, make the decisions and give the orders. That all clear?"

Sloan stood and looked at each of the three. He was nearly six feet tall, solidly built and carried his six-gun tied low on his leg as if he knew how to use it. Brownish gray hair spilled out from under a battered brown hat. His brown eyes studied them. Spur knew the lawman was ready for instant action. His hand hovered near the weapon as he waited for their responses. One man grunted assent. The bearded one shrugged. Agreement came from the other man Spur could not see.

"Tell the rest of your story, McCoy," Sheriff Sloan said. "Ain't saying I believe you, but ain't saying I don't neither."

Spur told him what happened, from his first hearing the shots to his attempt to stop the three

riders from leaving when he was shot. After Spur
had finished, one of the men walked up to the sheriff
and whispered to him.

It was Spur's first real look at the man. He was
short, about five feet six, and heavy at over a
hundred and eighty pounds. The fat man watched
Spur.

"Like we figured, Sheriff. The woman inside has
been stripped naked and raped and cut up some,
then half her head was shot off. Two kids in there,
both stabbed to death and their throats slashed. So
the whole family is deader than a day old buzzard
feast." He glared at Spur. "Leastwise we got one of
the bastards who done it!"

"Not a chance," Spur said. "I can prove who I am
and what I am, and . . ." He stopped. He couldn't
prove a thing! In that last river crossing his mount
had slipped and fallen and he went into the water.
His wallet with half his cash and his new identification card from Washington D.C. had been swept
downstream. There was no telegraph for two
hundred miles. He could not prove who he was
without waiting for a week to ten days for a letter!

"So prove it," the thin faced, black eyed man said.
"I say he can't prove nothing. We got all the damn
evidence that we need to convict!"

"For once I agree with you, Long. We take him
back to Twin Falls to stand trial for the deaths of
Ned Bailey, his wife and kids, as well as the rest of
all this."

Spur knew he had to talk his way out of this
mess. His six-gun was gone from his holster. The
Spencer leaned against the cabin out of reach. The
sheriff seemed like a fair man, maybe he had a
chance.

"Sheriff, I'm a lawman, a federal lawman. Get me

to a telegraph and I can prove it. I'm on my way to Twin Falls on government business."

"Sure, and I'm fucking President Grant!" The fat man shouted, his voice rising into a howling laugh.

"All I ask is a way to prove who I am," Spur said. "I'll gladly go to Twin Falls with you and you can send a letter to the nearest telegraph station and have them get my identity from Washington, D.C."

"Sounds reasonable," Sheriff Sloan said. "You just might be who you say. Course, then you might be one of the four killers we've been chasing since we left Twin Falls yesterday afternoon. The four held up a saloon owner, robbed him of five hundred dollars, then killed him when he went for his gun. We chased them out of town and lost them last night. They stayed at a small farm. By the time we got there this morning, they had raped the mother and daughter and killed the farmer."

"I've never been in Twin Falls before," Spur said.

"Mite hard to prove that," Sheriff Sloan said. "You do fit the general description, even your horse, hat and rifle match the killers. You could have come here, got yourself shot up and the other three left you behind so you wouldn't slow them down. I seen that happen before."

"Three horses rode out, check the prints," Spur said. "So where does that fifth man come from, the one dead by the outhouse?"

"Yeah, you got a point. Tolerable point. But like I said, he could have been a hired hand. Guess we should get you patched up a little better so you can ride back to town."

"No need for that, Sheriff," the bearded man said. He had drawn his hogsleg and cocked the hammer. "This Jasper ain't traveling much more than a hundred feet to that oak tree over there. Easy

Sheriff! Just lay your iron on the porch right there. We decided, the three of us. No sense dragging this killer all the way back to town. We'll have a little necktie party right here, on that oak. Save the county the cost of a trial and a hangman."

Sheriff Sloan turned slowly and looked at the other two men. "This one is crazy, we all know that. But, Hoffer, you're no fool. You know this evidence is circumstantial. Might not be true at all. You ain't going along with a wild man like Gabe Young, are you?"

"We decided, Sheriff," Hoffer said. "Hell, Abe, ease up a little. Ain't no damn leather off your saddle. Just a little old fashioned justice. An eye for an eye. We got him dead to rights!"

The sheriff scowled. "Boots, you going along with these idiots? Against the law to do this, Boots. You're usually a good, reliable man. Could get you in one hell of a lot of trouble if you go through with a lynching."

Boots shuffled his feet. He was twenty-eight, tall, gangling, with soft blond hair and a narrow face. He grinned with a lopsided tilt.

"Hell, Sheriff, we just having a little fun. Worked damn hard all week. Man's got to have a little fun."

"Damn, Boots, you still drunk? When in hell you going to sober up? You said you wouldn't drink until we got back." The sheriff stood there, hands on his hips.

"Now, Sheriff, don't you fret," Gabe Young said waving his six-gun. We deputies! We just upholding the law. Found us a murderer and we sentenced him. Now we gonna put him on his horse and watch the bastard stretch hemp! Nothing you can do about it, except watch. Move away from your six-gun and sit down. We got to tie you up till the fun is all over."

"But you can watch, Sheriff," Hoffer said. "Wouldn't deny you the enjoyment of watching a good hanging."

"Yeah, Sheriff," Long said. "Hanging is a right fun time for everybody." He laughed. "Hell it's fun for almost everybody." He kicked Spur in the kidney and laughed when he doubled up and rolled off the porch into the hot dust.

2

Gabe Young grabbed Spur by the shoulder and pulled him to his feet. As soon as he stood up some-one tied his hands behind him. Until that moment, Spur was sure he could get away from the four men. The sheriff would be a help. But the quickness of the hand tie ruined his chances.

He would have to kick the one with the gun.

Young moved back out of range of Spur's sudden flailing foot.

"You'll have to do better than that, McCoy!" Young shouted. He laughed softly. "Not a chance in hell that you're going to get out of this. So just take it easy, you murdering bastard! We want to do this right, snuff out your worthless life with a two foot drop! Yeah, this is getting better all the time!"

"You hang him, you know I'll come after you, Young," Sheriff Sloan said. "You're the instigator. You take a prisoner from me and I'll hunt you down and shoot your balls off just for fun and then you'll die so slow you'll be begging me . . ."

19

Young slammed the side of his six gun against Sheriff Sloan's head, toppling him into the dirt off the porch.

"Shut up, old man! Just shut up!"

"You sure this is the guy you saw busting out of the saloon?" Hoffer asked Young softly.

"Hell yes! I said so didn't I? You getting chicken feet here, Hoffer?"

"No. I just want to be sure you saw this one."

Boots came up and stared at Spur.

"Sure looks mean enough to kill them," Boots said, his drunk grin fading a little. He looked at Spur again, then nodded and went to his saddle for a rope. He came back with his lariat, a stiff throwing rope not much more than three-eighths of an inch in diameter but strong enough to stop a nine hundred pound steer.

"Need a bigger rope," Young said.

"Don't got one," Boots said.

Young spat on the ground, eyed the rope again. "Hail, it'll have to do. Tie a good hangman's knot with thirteen loops, and make sure it's done right."

"Don't know how," Boots said.

"Christ! I have to do it all?" Young shrilled.

He took the rope and tried to tie a hangman's knot. Three times he wound the rope and made the loop. It never came out right.

Hoffer watched him but threw up his hands when Young offered him the rope. At last they went to the sheriff.

"Old man," Gabe Young said. "You tie us a hangman's knot or I'm gonna shoot you in the leg. You savvy?"

"If I don't, even then make a noose for you?"

"We'll turn this Jasper loose and let him run for it

while we use him for target practice. Take your pick."

Sheriff Sloan waited for Hoffer to untie him, then took the rope. Young stood six feet in front of him with his six-gun aimed at the unarmed sheriff's chest.

"The hanging would be more humane, I guess," Sheriff Sloan said. He quickly fashioned a hangman's noose with thirteen loops around it and gave it to Young.

Young put his arm through the noose and pulled the free end. The rope slid through and tightened around his arm. Young grunted and motioned for the other two to move Spur toward the oak at the side of the small corral.

"McCoy!" the sheriff called. The trio stopped and turned. "Look, I'm sorry. This got out of hand. Any in-laws I can notify? Anything I can do?"

"Looks like you've done enough," Spur said nodding at the noose.

"I'll track these guys down," Sloan said. "Last thing I do I'll get them for you."

"Helps me a hell of a lot when I'm dead," Spur said.

The men pushed him toward the tree. Spur watched the sheriff a minute longer. He whispered some words, but Spur could not read his lips. The only word he caught was "noose." He turned and looked at the instrument of death that Boots carried. It was a small version of the hangman's noose since the rope was thin, but he could see nothing unusual. What did the sheriff mean?

"Bring his horse," Young said. "And take off the saddle. That's the way it's done."

Spur watched every move. There was simply no

chance. He could run, but they would chase him down and bring him back. He might get in one lucky kick but that still left two of them, and they all carried guns. Young was the one to go for, but he stayed well out of range. It took Young three tries to get the noose end of the rope thrown over the oak branch that jutted from the oak tree fifteen feet off the ground.

They dropped the noose down to the right height, then had to tie two lariats together, so the rope could be tied around a low branch on the tree.

It took all three of them to boost Spur onto the back of his horse. He sat facing backwards on the horse and Hoffer held the reins in front. There was no chance to surge away and ride out of danger. He would have tried it even backwards, but there was not a chance.

Spur looked at the swinging noose and felt sweat on his forehead. That was death staring at him. That loop of rope would strangle him if it didn't break his neck.

Hoffer rode up and slipped the noose over his head and pulled it snug. Spur could still breathe.

"Take up the slack," Hoffer directed Long. "The damned rope will stretch enough to give him a jolt when he hits bottom."

Spur looked and saw Boots holding his horse. Still no chance.

Hoffer rode away and Spur could feel the pressure on his neck as the horse under him shifted positions. Boots kept her from moving much.

Long and Hoffer rode up beside Spur. Both were grinning.

"McCoy, you bastard, you raping, murdering son of a bitch!" Young said. "Your life of crime is almost over. Anything you want to say to the assembled throng?'' Long giggled.

Spur stared at him a minute.

"You'll have to live with this, all three of you. I'm a United States lawman, and did not hurt anyone in this county. I only just arrived . . ."

Long hit him across the face with the back of his hand.

"Hell, I never did like long speeches." He took out a six inch sheath knife and nodded at Hoffer who sat his mount on the other side of Spur's horse. Hoffer took out a knife and grinned at Spur.

"Don't rightly care if you're a federal lawman or not," Hoffer said. "Might even be a mite relieved if you are, come to think. But what the hell, a hanging is a hanging. I love to go to hangings."

Spur watched both men, then looked at the way the rope looped over the limb and was tied off. It was a good job. He would not reach the ground.

He knew he would not live forever, but this seemed like a useless, senseless way to die. His life did not flash in front of him. Rather he concentrated on memorizing the faces of the three lynchers. If he ever had the chance he would haunt them as long as they lived!

Spur McCoy looked at Long. He could see the nature of the man. He was all bad, always had been, always would be until somebody killed him. There was a brief moment of recognition as Long accepted the fact that Spur was a lawman and that they had a certain kinship in living on the very edge of disaster and euphoria, never knowing which one would come next, but knowing that therein lay the thrill of living. The not knowing made every day a new challenge and a new thrill.

Then the spark died in Long's eyes.

"So long, asshole," he said and nodded at Hoffer.

Both men thrust their knives foward, slashing at the hindquarters of the horse. The mount bellowed in pain and rage, dug in her back hooves and her powerful rear quarters drove her forward.

Spur McCoy jolted off the horse and dropped to the end of the rope. The hemp stretched, and held.

3

Spur's mind was clear, sharp as he heard the mount bellow in rage and surge forward. He felt his body dragged off the horse's rump, felt the rope tighten around his neck more gradually than he had expected.

Then came the searing burning on his neck as he dropped to the end of the slack and the rope tore away flesh. His head rolled to the left and he felt the heavy knot on the right side of his neck.

For just an instant he realized his neck was not broken, but there was still strangulation that would kill him just as dead if not quite so quickly. The six or eight seconds seemed like an eternity. He saw the green of the tree overhead, knew his body was swinging on the rope. He remembered that the sheriff had tied the knot, had he done something to give Spur a chance? The sky was blue, he saw that. He heard a low laugh from one of the lynchers. A moment later it was too much effort to keep his eyes open.

Then it all faded and wavered, came back for a second, then it was gone in a blinding rush as the black clouds closed around him and Spur McCoy knew nothing else.

Gabe Long shrilled a long laugh. "Keeeeereist! Look at that! His damn neck must be broke, and his eyes are bulging. Will his tongue stick out? Never seen me many hangings, leastways, not up close like this. Keeeeeeeeeeeeriest! Look at that!"

Boots stared at the man hanging by his neck. The last of his alcohol fog evaporated and he looked at the hanged man, then at the three of them and closed his eyes. He'd been a part of it! Damn! How drunk had he been? And for how long? There would be hell to pay for this. He just hoped that he wouldn't have to move to another state. Not another time. Goddamnit, he was swearing off the booze . . . again.

Josh Hoffer watched the body swaying back and forth, then saw it turn slowly until it had made an entire circuit. Hell, the guy had to be dead by now. Hoffer had never seen a hanging before and he wasn't overjoyed by this one. It sure was a new experience!

"Let's get the hell out of here!" Hoffer said. He looked at Young who stood at arms length from the body. McCoy's boots hung two feet off the ground. "I'm going," Hoffer said. He walked back to where his horse was tied. Then he remembered the sheriff. He hurried over to him, untied his hands but kept the lawman's six-gun.

"Don't want you doing nothing foolish, now, Sheriff. You get yourself up on your horse and we're riding out of here."

By the time they were mounted up, Boots and Young had joined them. Young wanted to use the corpse for target practice, but the others ignored him and they rode out.

They had watched the body twitch for two or three minutes. When they were half a mile away, the sheriff turned.

"You can shoot me in the back if you want, but I'm going to go back and cut him down. He deserves a decent burial, at least." The sheriff turned and rode away. When he realized the trio was not going to interfere or shoot him down, he rode harder and came up to the oak tree in a rush. He looked behind him and saw the trio of riders vanish over the ridge, then rode up to McCoy and slashed the lariat in half, letting the man's body crumple into the dirt.

Sheriff Sloan dropped off his horse and loosened the noose around McCoy's neck and stared hard at him.

Spur McCoy coughed.

Sloan grinned and sat beside him, taking the noose away, staring at the ugly rope burn on McCoy's neck.

The sheriff bent and listened to McCoy's heart beat through his chest. He laughed softly.

"Yeah, McCoy, don't know if you can hear me or not, but you should pull through. Tying that hangman's knot was our only chance. I did the Murphy knot. It puts most of the pressure on the side of the head, and if it's tied right, is guaranteed not to break the man's neck and not even strangle him.

"Sure it cuts off the blood supply to part of the brain, but not all of it. That's the secret. You look damn dead, but you really ain't."

McCoy coughed again. The sheriff cut the rope off his hands and wiped his face with a wet kerchief.

He listened. The man was breathing deep and regularly. Sheriff Sloan slapped Spur's face lightly, then harder. There was no response. He took his canteen off his saddle and sloshed water over the secret agent's face and he snorted, shook his head and groaned.

"That's better, McCoy. Come on, snap out of it. You're not half dead yet. Want you to walk down to the porch so I can get you back to normal."

McCoy groaned again, lifted one hand to his face and then his eyes fluttered, opened, closed against the sun and Sloan shaded his eyes. This time they came open and turned toward the sheriff.

"Right, McCoy, you're still alive. Not many men get hanged and live to tell about it. Saw it happen once before. You won't be able to talk for a while, maybe not for a day or two. Don't worry about it, voice should come back. Might be a little different sounding though." He shrugged. "Hell anything is better than dead."

He got Spur a drink of water from the well. Spur tried to drink, spit out the first try, then sipped a small bit at a time and got some down.

The sheriff helped Spur sit up, then to stand. They walked slowly down to the cabin and sat on the porch. It took almost twenty minutes to move the hundred yards.

Sheriff Sloan lolled on the porch as if he didn't have a thing in the world to do.

"Damn glad they asked me to tie the knot for them. I was hoping they couldn't tie a real hangman's knot. Not many people can, and it's against the law when you come right down to it. So I tied them Murphy's knot. I was trying to tell you not to worry so much when they led you away, but not much I could do. I didn't want them to look too close at the noose. Whole idea is to fix it so the rope will pull through, but it binds against itself so the pressure isn't as great and course with that little rope, that knot itself isn't big enough to break a man's neck. So you worry about strangling and cutting off blood to the brain.''

Sloan looked at Spur. "Time. Time is what we have lots of now. Don't want to move too fast. Them three will think I'm back here doing the burying on five or six bodies, so it should take some time. It's a good long day's ride back to Twin Falls from here. We'll let them get back and situated. Then when you feel like it, we can move.''

Spur looked up waved his hand to get the sheriff's attention, then tried to say something. The croak that came out surprised Spur more than Sheriff Sloan.

"Yep, sounds about right. You're bound to do that for a day or two. Good sign, though, McCoy. Shows that the voice box is still there and functioning. Now all we have to do is let mother nature fine tune the instrument.''

The sheriff went for more water from the well, gave Spur another small drink, then checked the leg wound. He went into the death house and came back with a bed sheet and a tablet and two pencils.

"Figure you might want to give me some more details about yourself and your job out here,'' Sloan said. He passed the tablet to Spur who took a pencil and began writing.

"Yes, thanks. I am a Secret Service Agent. You probably never heard of me, but you can check me out by wiring to General Wilton D. Halleck, in care of Capital Investigations, Washington, D.C.''

The sheriff read it and nodded.

"Don't see as how I have any real need to do that. I size up folks quick like. You say you're a lawman for the Federal people, that's good enough for me.

Why you coming to Twin Falls? We only got about a thousand people in the whole town, maybe fifteen hundred in Twin Falls county.''

"Can't tell you yet, Sheriff. If I need your help I'll give you all the details . . . later.''

"Fine. Like I say I figure people out quick.'' He stood. "I better get at my gardening, or I'll never get finished.'' He went to the barn, found a shovel and came back.

An hour later the sheriff had dug two shallow graves and buried the two men. He went up near the oak tree and dug again, then carried the blanket wrapped body of the woman and then the two children up and lay them in the same grave. He was done well before dark.

Spur had been up and walking. He carried his head at a strange angle because his neck felt better that way. When the sheriff came back, he looked in the house again and found some ointment and made some bandages from the sheet, then treated Spur's neck and his leg. He wrapped both with yards of the white three-inch strips of sheet, then tore up some more and rolled them up and stuffed them in his saddle bags.

The sheriff found fresh bread in the house, some nearly melted butter and a jar of preserves. Behind the barn he located the milk cow and they had bread and jam and fresh, warm milk for supper.

Twice more Spur had tried to talk, but his voice croaked and wheezed. The third time the words were understandable, but still tinged with strange creaks and whistles.

"By morning you'll be feeling better,'' the sheriff said. "You need a good night's rest, then with some breakfast in our bellies, we'll strike out for Twin Falls.''

* * *

By noon the next day, Spur's voice had almost returned to normal. It had a deeper sound now, more resonant, and the sheriff said it might stay that way forever, or it could slip back to the tone it had previously.

They stopped at the family where the farmer had been killed and were given a late dinner. The women were quiet, polite but reserved. Spur did not blame them. Spur put down enough beef stew and vegetables and chunks of good wheat bread to feed three men. He was feeling better. He spoke only when he had to, and did not trust his voice.

They rode late into the afternoon, then it turned dusk and they could see the kerosene lamps glowing ahead in Twin Falls.

"Sheriff, tell me about those three men," Spur said.

"Whatever they done is my responsibility," Sloan said. "Wish I could charge them with murder, but that would be hard to do, you walking around and all. I can charge them with *attempted* murder, but our judges don't hold much with that kind of legal maneuvering."

"They think they killed me," Spur said slowly. "I just might be able to scare them to death. Tell me about them."

"Thought you had an assignment here?"

"Do, but it can wait a day or two. Tell me."

"Boots Dallman is the blond guy. Surprised he went along with it, but then figured out he was still drunk. Never got him to go on a posse before. Probably wouldn't have gone if he wasn't pied right up to the gills that afternoon. I needed him, needed at least four against four.

"Dallman is a family man, wife and two kids.

Lives outside of town to the south about five miles on a little spread. Homestead I think. He works sometimes for the Box B ranch, a big outfit. Boots is a good man. He just got carried away, then was in over his head. Gabe Young had him scared shitless out there."

"I had the same feeling," Spur said, the whistles lessening. "What about Young?"

"Been in trouble in half of the state, mostly between here and Boise. Drifter, gambler, gun for hire sometimes. A killer who doesn't care who goes down. I only took him because he can use those guns of his. I had to have some firepower. He's maybe twenty-five or six years old. Figure he'll never make thirty.

"Other man is Joshua Hoffer, nearing fifty now. A merchant in town but not exactly a lily-white character. He is not a pillar in the church or the community. Has a good General Mercantile, and you can find things you need there they don't even stock in Boise."

"Bloodthirsty little bastard," Spur said, the croak coming back into his voice.

"True, this time. Generally he's harmless." The sheriff watched Spur as they rode toward the outskirts of the town.

"Lawman or no, I'm going to be watching you. There are no legal charges I can bring against the three that will stick."

"Fair enough, Sheriff."

"So don't go off half cocked. I'd hate to have to hang you for murder."

"Sheriff, I'd hate to have to hang for murder. Way I look at it, if one or two of these guys has an *accident* it would be mighty hard to prove that it was murder."

They stopped a block from the only hotel in town, it was a three story affair over a saloon. One door led into the hotel, the other door to the drinking, gaming, fancy-lady establishment.

"McCoy, you had a rough time, but you've alive. It's better than being dead. I helped keep you alive. Don't make me move against you."

".Sheriff, you ever been hanged?"

The big man on the black horse shook his head slowly.

"Then don't be telling me what I can and can't do, not until you've walked at least a mile in the boots of a man who has been!"

4

Sheriff Abe Sloan laughed softly to himself.

"I know you're right, McCoy. But I still don't want to hang you. You bury any of the three of them in my county, and I'll put you on trial for murder. Don't believe that I won't."

The two men stared at each other for a minute, understanding the other's point of view, feeling a strange camaraderie that set them apart from normal mortals. At last they both smiled, nodded, then they continued their ride into town.

The sheriff took Spur up the back stairs of the hotel and put him in a room, then went downstairs and registered him.

When he came back he gave Spur the key. "Looks like the county owes you one night's lodging," Sloan said. "Best damn bed in the place." He hesitated. "You, ah . . . You need anything else?"

"Just some supper, maybe a bath and then a good night's sleep. Thanks for that Murphy knot. I owe you a rather large favor one of these days."

"That you do. I'll stop by Doc Rawson's place and have him come up and look you over. He'll cuss and fume and rant about my sloppy doctoring, but he was the one who trained me two years ago. I had been losing shot up suspects. He showed me how to stop the bleeding at least."

Sloan paused at the door, his big, rough hands turning his hat by the brim. When he completed one full turn, he glanced up.

"McCoy, you need anything, you just give a call. I'm damn glad you're still alive." Sheriff Sloan put on his hat and hurried out the door and down the hall.

Spur watched him go. He would be as careful as he could about not *burying anybody* in Twin Falls county. Outside the county line might be another matter. He liked the big, rough and ready sheriff. He was the kind most towns in the West needed: tough enough to handle the job, but smart enough to know when to be gentle. Most towns couldn't find the right kind of man.

A half hour later Doc Rawson came and stared at Spur a moment, then sat on the bed and rubbed his face. The medic was small and wiry, wore a black suit, carried a black bag and had dried blood stains on his shirt sleeves. He swore as he unwrapped the bloody bandage from Spur's neck.

"Rope burn?" Doc Rawson said.

Spur nodded. "I'd be grateful if you didn't let it get around about me or about the little scrape I got into that produced that rope problem," Spur said.

"Abraham told me about the same thing . . . the sheriff." He touched the wound and the side of Spur's head. The fingers hurt where he pressed on his head.

"Bruise up there. You actually were hung?"

"That's not a thing a man brags about, Doc."

"At least not in this world. Was it a Murphy's knot?"

"That's what Sheriff Sloan called it. He did the tying."

"Then hurried like hell back and cut you down before you strangled! That old son of a bitch!" Spur could feel the admiration and respect come through the doctor's words. He probed with a pair of pliers looking things, pulled free some stuck cloth and nodded.

"Hell, we'll have you up and around in a week or so." He applied something to the neck wound and Spur reacted. "Hurts, like hell, don't it? My old mother used to say if it didn't hurt, it wasn't helping any. Any rate it's a hell of a lot better than the alternative . . . dead."

He clipped off some curled up skin, trimmed another place and then asked Spur to talk. He did.

"Your voice has come back quickly. Don't use it too much in the next few days. No loud hollering, hog calling, or bellowing at fancy women."

Spur grinned.

"Thought I would hit something familiar sooner or later. Understand you could use a telegraph?"

"Right."

"I use the one down at Salt Junction, in Utah now and then. Made arrangements with the operator down there. I send in my message by mail direct to him. It's just north of the Great Salt Lake. Have to send it by mail to Pocatello on the stage. That's six days. Then six days coming back. Figure two weeks. That help you any?"

"I hope not. My plans call for me being on that stage myself before that long. But thanks."

The doctor looked at his leg, swore again, doused the wound with alcohol and brought a surprised shriek of pain from Spur.

"If it don't hurt . . ." the humorist medic said. Then he went to work and dug out the slug which for some reason had not gone all the way through. Spur gritted his teeth and pounded the bed once with his hand. The pain was twice as bad as the alcohol on the raw flesh, and it lasted longer.

"Missed most of the bone," Doc said. "But sure did cut up some of your leg. Gonna hurt like hell for two days. Advise you to try some Southern Comfort or Old Crow whiskey as a pain killer. Course I want you to stay off it for a week. By then you'll be in shape to get back to work. Whatever that might be."

Spur paid him twenty dollars for the surgery and house call. Doc Rawson looked at the twenty dollar bill and smiled.

"If I had more patients like you, Spur McCoy I could retire rich in five years. Usually I only charge two dollars to deliver a baby, fifty cents for a house call. Trouble is most nobody has any money to pay. I do get chickens, and garden vegetables and fruit in season, though."

Spur thanked him, promised he'd be to his office every two days so he could check the bandages, and closed the door. Spur looked at himself in the wavy mirror over the wash basin. He scrubbed his face, chest and arms, combed his hair and found he could hold his head straight if he tried. He put a red kerchief over the white bandage, slipped into a clean shirt and went down to the dining room for the last lean, rare steak from the kitchen. By the time he got back to his room it was almost nine o'clock. He had just taken off his shirt when someone knocked on the door.

He frowned, picked up his Colt .45 and thumbed back the hammer. He held the six-gun behind the door as he opened it a crack.

One pretty blue eye and a narrow slice of pouting red mouth looked back at him. Spur edged the door open farther and saw the whole girl. She was barely five feet tall, had silver blonde hair piled high up on her head and wore too much rouge and lipstick to be an honest woman.

"Abe Sloan has a message for you," she said, her blue eyes dancing, looking him up and down and not showing disappointment.

"A message?"

"I can't deliver it out here in the hall."

"Oh, come in." He held the door open, then left it a foot from being closed.

"My name is Clarice, that's French. My name means little brilliant one." She smiled and closed the door, then leaned against it.

"You had a message," Spur said smiling now.

"Yes. Mr. Sloan says he knows that you have been hurt, and that you may need something to take your mind off the pain, and that he welcomes you to Twin Falls and wishes you success on your assignment here."

"That's very kind of Sheriff Sloan . . . ."

"He said you might be difficult. I used to dance, did you know that? I was pretty good. But my costume kept falling off, so pretty soon I built that into my act, and changed jobs and before long, all of my clothes were falling off and I was a smashing success."

She took his hand, sat him on the bed and then

humming a scratchy tune, began to dance for him.

He stood. "Clarice, there is really no reason . . ."

She stopped dancing and stamped her small foot.
As she did the strap that held up the top of her dress
came loose, fell from her shoulder and dropped so
low it revealed one large breast with a brown areola
and red nipple.

"Just sit back down and please don't interrupt
again," Clarice said. She continued dancing,
ignoring the broken strap and the exposed breast.
The dance picked up in speed and in the small room
there was little space. She did a series of quick steps
and the other side of her dress dropped down to her
waist revealing the other breast.

Clarice clapped her hands and hummed the tune.
Three steps later she did a small jump and the dress
she once wore slid over her slender hips and dropped
to the floor. She wore only thin, pink panties that
barely covered her crotch.

Clarice turned and pranced toward him.

"This is not one of those dances where you can't
touch the performers. In fact touching is
encouraged. Kissing is expected, fondling is
demanded."

She sat beside him.

"Think I could take your mind off your troubles
tonight?"

"Clarice, I'm sure you could, tonight or any night.
But I am really tired, and I do hurt."

She shushed him and put her hands on his
shoulders and pushed him down on the bed, lying on
top of him. She was careful not to touch his neck or
his hurt leg.

"I'm a specialist on tired, and I'm not too heavy
to smash you down. I'll do all the work, all you have
to do is have fun and enjoy."

"Just pure sex?"

"Just fun fucking!" Her face came toward his. She lowered herself more and more until her lips touched his and pulled away.

"Kissing?"

"Some do, some don't," he said.

She laughed and kissed him. "I do." She kissed him again, her tongue exploring his open mouth. When the kiss ended, she smiled.

"You have an insistent third leg growing down there." Clarice smiled and lay on his chest for a moment. "I am sorry you were hurt. I'm not sure how or why, it doesn't matter. I just want to kiss it and make it feel better."

"Somehow I think you'll do just that," Spur said.

"Good! First, let me get your boots off, and then these pants. I'm really anxious to get a look at your good parts."

She undressed him slowly, carefully, not allowing any pain to his leg. When he was naked, she stood over him and beckoned.

"Into the next room. There's a connecting door. Everything has been arranged."

She opened the door and inside the next room he saw that it was twice as large as the one he had been in. There was a large bed, two soft chairs, and a steaming portable bathtub and three extra pails of hot water.

"I want you clean and smelling like a whole pine forest! I love the pine forests. And we'll be careful not to get your bandages wet. The sheriff warned me about that."

She smiled at him, her soft silver blonde hair loose now and falling half way down her neck.

"Come on, slow poke. You first in the tub. Step in and sit down with one foot, and we'll put your bandaged leg up on the side.''

He stepped in on his good leg and sat down,
yowling at the hotness of the water. Clarice
laughed and dumped in half a bucket of cold, then
began washing him, lathering him with two large
cakes of pine-scented soap. She washed his face and
his shoulders, all the time careful not to get the neck
bandage wet. Then she worked lower and found a
strange swelling just under the water.

She bent lower and pushed one of her breasts into
Spur's mouth and he chewed on it.

Quickly then she stood, stripped down the pink,
silk panties and moved toward him. Gently she sat
down facing him, lowering herself on his stiff penis
until she had enveloped all of him. Then she shrieked
in victory and began bouncing up and down on him.

Spur felt himself building quickly to a climax and
before he wanted to, he exploded and jolted her
upward with each thrust, then sank back below the
water as she leaned forward and brushed his lips
with hers.

"Sweetheart, that was nice, but too common.
We're just getting started. Do you know of the one
hundred and thirty-seven traditional Japanese
positions for having sex, six of them are in a
bathtub? I bet you didn't know that.''

She lifted away from him and went on bathing
him, scrubbing all except his injured calf, and when
she was through, there was not a spot of water on
either bandage.

Spur touched her breasts and she looked at him.

"You didn't get your turn.''

"I don't get a turn, I'm working. You know that.''

"With me you still get a turn.''

"Later. Right now we need to get you out of that

tub and rubbed dry and stuffed under those silk sheets on the best bed in town. I've never been in this room before. The owner reserves it for extremely important people. Then again he isn't against making a few extra dollars. Why is the sheriff going to all this trouble for you?"

"I was hoping, Clarice, that you could tell me."

"Not a clue. I'm not paid to think, and most people say I'm not very smart but that I have a cute little ass and a pussy that just won't ever get tired of getting filled full. So what do I know?"

"You know plenty, and your dumb act is a cover-up for the real you. I just wished that I had the time to uncover you."

Clarice laughed. She spun around naked in front of him and he saw how her breasts swung out delight-fully.

"Spur McCoy, I'm about as uncovered as a girl can get. Do you like what you see?"

"What I see and what I hear."

She led him to the bed and folded down the silk sheets. Spur could not remember silk sheets but back there sometime in New York he was sure his mother had them just for show, and on the guest room bed.

He slid between them and held them up for her. She snuggled against him and sniffed.

"You're a pine tree!"

He tucked the silk sheet around her. "Have you heard about anything crooked going on by the sheriff?"

"No. He's pure as the driven snow. I mean it. I offered it to him a dozen times, and he says no, but thanks. He's got a wife and he wouldn't cheat on her, not ever. He's tough, and he can shoot. I saw him kill two robbers once in a saloon. Just as cool and cold as hell! Next day he helped deliver a baby when Doc was out of town.''

He lay there a moment, then moved his hand over one of her breasts and massaged it gently.

"I bet you know how to go around the world. I'm tired, but with you directing my tour, I bet we can get at least all the way across Europe and around to India somewhere.''

Clarice laughed "You're going to China or I don't know my business. First we have to do New York. You ever been to New York?''

"I was born and grew up there," Spur said.

Clarice showed him a New York he had never suspected.

Well before India, Spur McCoy went down for the count. He never answered the bell for the seventh bare knuckled contest and Clarice declared herself the winner. She snuggled down in the silk sheets dreaming she was a princess, and went to sleep with one arm across Spur McCoy's broad chest.

5

Clarice sat on the bed, hugging her knees to her bare breasts and watched Spur McCoy.

"You're a pretty man," she said. "What a fine body you have." She giggled. "And you certainly do know how to use it! You almost filled me up and made me want to stop, almost but not quite. I don't ever remember that happening before."

McCoy pulled on a pair of town pants, soft brown ones with a crease down the front.

"Oh, Sheriff Sloan said to tell you, case you was interested, that Gabe Young hit town, changed horses, bought a bottle and lit out down the stage road toward Boise. That was about half an hour after he got into town."

Spur sat down beside her, reached in and kissed one bouncing breast, then the other one.

"Thanks, you saved me half a day." He pulled off the town pants and switched to denims, then put on a blue shirt and a brown leather vest. He tugged his boots on over two pair of soft cotton socks.

"You're going after him?" she asked.

Spur nodded.

"Damn! That means I got to go back to work."

Spur was turning his head slowly from one side to the other. It was stiff and sore, burned like Hades, but there wasn't anything he could do about that. He knew he couldn't afford to get in a situation where his injuries would slow him down. It could be a deadly problem.

Clarice stood on the bed. She was naked. She leaned over and put her arms around Spur's shoulders and looked him right in the eye.

"You come back, nice man. Last night was something special for me. It wasn't work at all. You keep your body from getting cut up or shot any more!"

Spur kissed her and smiled.

"Do my best. I better get moving. Leaving my gear here. You're welcome to stay. Not just sure when I'll be back."

Spur slung his saddle bags over his shoulder, hoisted his Spencer and went out the door. He had a cold trail to follow, so he better get moving.

At the livery he picked up his horse where the sheriff had taken it, paid for the keep and needed help in saddling the big black. She was sturdy and deep chested, and could outlast three mules. Ten minutes later he was on the stage road northwest.

He had never been to Boise, capital of the Territory of Idaho.

Spur asked about Gabe Young and the livery man knew him. Said Gabe was a sharp man when it came to horse trading. Talked the livery man out of a white stallion he'd been saving. Traded him a half blown sorrel and twenty dollars for him. Livery man said Young wanted the horse because it matched his high crowned white hat.

Spur rode. His neck pained him more than he thought possible, a continual dull ache and sharp pains shooting into his head. He stopped at the first farm house near the main road.

The woman who came to the door eyed him suspiciously. She said she'd seen the man on the white horse. He rode past the previous day sometime. Didn't stop. Spur thanked her and pushed on.

It was almost noon when he turned down a half mile lane toward a small ranch. Just as he got to the well house fifty feet from the side door of the small frame residence, a shotgun boomed birdshot over his head.

"Far enough!" A man's voice bellowed. "State your name and your business, or move down the road!"

"Spur McCoy is my name and I'm tracking an outlaw who rode past here on a white horse."

"You a lawman?"

"Yes. Any help you can give me would be appreciated."

"Oh, sorry. Step down and come in for some victuals. Wife is just ready to set up dinner."

A man came from the side door of the house carrying an old Greener double barreled shotgun. He still had one live round.

Spur got down slowly and kept his hands well away from his holster.

"You chasing Gabe Young, I'd figure," the rancher said. He wore overalls, and long johns but no shirt, even though it was June. "Bastard was here. Offered the sonofabitch a bed for the night and he took it. Sometime during the night he broke the lock on my eldest daughter's room and raped her. She's still all broke up about it. Don't know if she'll ever be the same. She was really a fine girl, promised to a guy over a section. Now the wedding is off, of course."

"You should ride into town and file a complaint with Sheriff Sloan. He will be interested."

"Might just do that." The man paused, wiped a rough hand over his sun-weathered face. "Yep, I might just do that. Won't help my daughter any, though." He stared at the barn for a minute, then waved Spur foward.

"Come in, come in. Meet the family. We're having fried chicken and biscuits and gravy for dinner. Hope you're hungry. Wife makes the best pot of coffee this side of Denver."

An hour later Spur was on his way. The hand drawn map he had picked up at the Mercantile before he left Twin Falls, showed the route to Boise was 145 miles. The stage road followed the Snake River downstream much of the way. He went across a ferry run by a family called Glenn. They had been moving people across the river at that point for years. People called it Glenn's Ferry.

The trail led more northerly then. Spur tried to maintain forty miles a day. Somehow he missed the stage, but it was just as well, since he had to check with ranchers and small settlements to make sure that Young had passed through.

He had, and seemed to leave a trail a dozen axe handles wide. Either he had no fear or a death wish hoping someone would find him.

The fourth day Spur's leg began to bleed. He made it into town just after noon and hobbled into a doctor's office. The medic looked at the leg and laughed.

"You come in from Twin Falls and old Doc Rawson wrapped up that leg, I'd bet a dollar!"

"Right, but no bet. Why did it start bleeding again?"

"You probably pushed it too fast. You young guys always seem to be in a rush for some reason."

The medic treated Spur's leg, taking a dozen stitches with some heavy black thread and told him to come back in a week for a cheekup.

Then Spur took off his neckerchief.

"Better take a look at this, too."

When the medic had the bandage off he swore.

"Never seen but one like that before. Must have been a small rope to gouge into your flesh that deep. Damn! You could get infection in there easy. You should be in bed somewhere."

"No time, Doc. Put some of that salve or something on it. Doc Rawson didn't seem too worried."

"Naturally, it ain't his neck!"

The doctor fussed and worked for fifteen minutes, then bandaged up the ugly wound.

"Like I said, you should be in bed resting. Give your body a chance to heal itself."

"Soon as I have time, Doc." Spur gave the man a ten dollar eagle gold coin. "Appreciate it if you don't tell anybody about my neck. Little piece of business I need to do in town."

"Guy who hung you is here?"

"Didn't say that, Doc. So don't you."

Out on the street, Spur talked with a friendly barkeep. He knew Gabe Young.

"The man is a scoundrel and a worthless no-good. Lives with a woman up the street a ways. Small yellow house with a white picket fence on the corner. You can't miss it if you try."

"Thanks, I better get up there. I owe Young some money and I want to pay him before he comes looking for me. He can get nasty that way."

Spur finished his beer and went out the door. It was four blocks to the yellow house on the corner with a white picket fence. Spur watched it for a minute, and saw three men go up the walk and into the house. All three looked like hard cases.

Spur sat down next to a big maple tree and watched the house. A half hour later the same three men came out with Gabe Young leading them. They walked downtown.

McCoy followed them from well back. None of them wore guns. They were armed when they went into the small house. Curious. In the small downtown area they separated. Two of them went into the Boise Home Bank. The other pair leaned against the outside, watching the people going by, looking at wagons and riders. One stood near the front door and a second by the door on the side street.

Were the four planning a bank robbery? Seemed like it. Spur started moving foward, then stopped. No guns. They were just looking over the place, working out what they had to do.

The two men came out of the bank one after the other and all four went down the street along the side door. They were walking one possible escape route. These guys must be experienced at bank robbery. They certainly were planning it out.

At the far corner they split, each going different directions. Spur walked back to the hotel dining room. It was closed until five that afternoon. He climbed to the third floor and put his key in the door lock. Someone came up behind him quickly and he turned, his hand on his six-gun.

"Don't move your hand, sir, or I'll shoot," a woman in front of him said. She was wearing brown, had brown hair and a stern face and held a .25 caliber six-gun aimed at him as if she knew how to use it.

"I don't shoot many women," Spur said relaxing, but she kept the gun covering him.

"Open your door and back in slowly all the way to the window," she said.

Spur shrugged. He had never seen the woman. She was young, attractive more than pretty, with a ripe, full figure.

"Just back up and don't talk," she said.

Spur backed into the room to the window. She came in, closed the door and kept the key.

"Take your weapon out and lay it on the floor, carefully."

He did.

"Now, slide it over to me on the floor with your foot."

Spur obeyed.

"Now that I'm harmless you can put away the hogsleg."

She smiled faintly, but little humor showed in her face. Gray eyes studied him.

"You've been asking a lot of questions about Gabe, Gabe Young. Why?"

"I owe him some money."

"Liar. Nobody owes Gabe money. He makes them pay quickly. Why are you asking questions about him? Why were you watching our house, and following him?"

"He's wanted in Twin Falls for murder. I'm a bounty hunter."

"More lies. You're no bounty man. I lived with one for two years before somebody killed him. You don't have the edge, the anger, the stomach for the job. Why?"

"He is wanted in Twin Falls for attempted murder."

"That charge won't get to trial in Idaho. Why are you hounding him? I know everything Gabe's ever done."

"Two days ago he raped a sixteen year old girl just outside of Twin Falls."

"That's possible. He uses lots of women, but he's always gentle and thoughtful with me."

She put the pistol down and sat on the side of the bed. "You don't know Gabe like I do. His father was a drunk. Never provided, gambled, worked only when he had to, and beat Gabe from the time he was big enough to make a fist. Taught him to fight back. He's been fighting ever since.

"When he was thirteen his mother taught him all about sex, she raped him every night his father wasn't home, five or six times a week. He soon hated her.

"When he was fourteen he was big enough and strong enough to lie in wait for his father. He clubbed him half to death, went inside and cut up his mother's breasts, then ran away from home. He's told me he hates women because of his mother, and he hates men for what his father did to him for so many years."

"Blaming others won't help him."

"I've tried to help. A minister tried. Two judges tried, then sentenced him. He broke out of jail. He's had three names in the past two years."

"Now he's going to rob the bank, the Boise Home bank. He was checking it over today."

"He's an expert at robbing banks. He has never been caught. That's how we live from day to day, on other people's money."

She brushed brown hair back from her eyes. "I wish I could stop him, but I can't. I'm tied to him now. If I tried to leave him he would kill me."

Slowly Spur took the kerchief from his neck. Edges of the wound showed around the bandage.

"Ever see what happens to a man when he gets hung, Mrs. Young?"

"I'm not married to Gabe. No, I never have. Were you . . . Gabe lynched you, and you lived?"

"Yes. I have a wound that will leave a scar for the rest of my life."

"That's another reason I have to help you." She stood and took off her light jacket, then began unbuttoning her calico dress that pinched in at her waist and swept the floor.

"I will do anything for you, Spur McCoy, if you will ride away and leave Gabe alone." The buttons came open and the fabric parted revealing a white camisole over her full breasts.

"I am not a loose woman, Mr. McCoy. It takes all of my strength to do this, but I will, for my man. Do you understand?"

"Yes, but I will make no deals with you about Gabe."

She let the dress top fall to her hips, then lifted off the frilly camisole. Her big breasts bounced and jiggled from her motions. Already their red nipples were enlarged with hot blood. Her pink areolas were large and tempting.

She walked toward him, smiling, her breasts jiggling.

"I can be very good for you, Spur. I can satisfy you, make you feel wonderful. I'll do anything you want to. You can put it in me wherever you want!"

She stood in front of him and massaged his crotch.

"I can never have children. God cursed me when

Gabe burned down a church and stole the collection. He cursed me and Gabe cursed me and I have to help him however I can. I still love him, and I always will. So if you harm Gabe, you're hurting me too, don't you understand?''

Spur cupped her breasts and kissed each, then he pushed her away. She was furious, tried again, grabbed him around his chest and ground her crotch against his. Gently Spur unlocked her hands and moved away from her.

She screamed, her voice full of hatred and fury. She turned lunged for the .25 caliber revolver she had left on the bed. She caught it and turned, but Spur slapped it away just as she fired. The bullet smashed the dresser mirror. Spur grabbed the gun and pushed her down on the bed.

"Get dressed and get out of here!" he said harshly. "You sound as sick as your man is!"

She sobbed on the bed a moment, then sat up, slowly pulled on her camisole and then lifted her dress and put it on and buttoned it.

"I'll keep the hardware. Now get out of here and don't come back. If you want to help your man, get him out of town before he tries to rob the bank."

Spur walked behind her until she had left by the side door. He watched her moving down the street until she was out of sight. Then he went back to the hotel clerk, told him he had some trouble in room 303 but wanted to continue to be registered there. He wanted to rent a second room where he would sleep, but did not want it to show on the books. For a two dollar gold piece the clerk decided he could break the rules just this once.

6

Gabe Young had been drinking most of the afternoon and evening. He was bored with drink and with gambling. He searched for Alice and caught her wrist.

"Upstairs, whore!" he bellowed.

Half the men in the room guffawed.

Alice tried to slap him but he caught her hand, then let go of it, grabbed a fistful of breast and tugged her forward.

"At least he knows what to hold onto!" Alice shrieked trying to make something positive out of her humiliation. She had always demanded to be treated as a lady, even when she was playing the role of a dance hall girl/upstairs whore.

Young let go of her breast, picked her up and slung her over his shoulder like a sack of wheat and carried her up the open stairs and down the hall to the biggest room. It was the *Three Dollar Bed*. He dropped her on the mattress and Alice rolled to the other side and held out her hand.

"Three dollars, big spender," she said. "Cash on the butt before the fucking."

Young laughed, fished out a five dollar gold piece and gave it to her. She slid it into a small purse in the top dresser drawer and began to unbutton her dress.

"I'll do it!" Young growled. He grabbed her, tied her hands behind her back. Then he used a kerchief and tied it around her mouth in a gag so she could little more than mumble words.

"Now, we'll get rid of them fancy-smancy clothes," Long said. He preened his full black beard and stared at her a minute from his black eyes. The ever present toothpick in his mouth pointed upward and he drew a sheath knife from leather at his waist. The blade was six inches long, honed so sharp he could shave with it. Now he used it to tease Alice's chin.

She gurgled something. Young slapped her face.

"Goddamn woman!" he bellowed. "You're all alike. You push and demand and order us, and just because you're smaller than us and soft and pretty you make us do it!"

He sat on the bed and nodded. His eyes glazed and he seemed to be in another world. Then he nodded again and opened his fly. His penis came out, stiff and hard.

"Yes. Yes, I'll do it for you, Mommie. We just did it last night. Do I have to again?"

He listened to some unspoken words, then his head bobbed and he gently opened the buttons down her bodice and spread back the cloth so Alice's breasts popped out.

His hands massaged them gently, tenderly, his head nodding as he listened to a voice Alice could not hear. He bent and nuzzled her breasts, then licked them and sucked one into his mouth. He chewed on it for a moment, then came away.

"Yes, Mommie. I can. Don't . . . don't hit me!"

With the knife he slit the side of the dress from the bodice opening to the bottom of the skirt and spread it back. Then the knife cut through more fabric until the knee-length drawers were cut off Alice and she lay there naked before him.

Gabe's eyes went blank for a moment as he stared at Alice.

"You want to be on top again, Mommie? No, no. We did it that way last night. Oh, darn! darn! darn! All right."

He lay down beside Alice, rolled her over on top of him and she watched intently to see what he wanted her to do. When it became obvious, she helped him enter her and then she lowered on his shaft.

"Oh, yes, that is nice!" Alice tried to say through the gag around her mouth. She was aware at once that he never heard her. His eyes were blank again, like black holes, as he listened to a different voice from his foggy memory. She had no real understanding of what was happening. But she had heard about Gabe Young. The girls said not to do anything to make him mad. He had hurt a girl one night.

Now she performed as well as she could and when he climaxed she started to lift off him but Gabe stopped her.

"I'm bigger now, Mommie. Lots stronger. And with this knife I have you can't slap me around the way you used to. Some day I'll make you sorry for all this, Mommie. Maybe even today!"

He pushed her off him to the side of the bed, sat up and caught hold of the sharp knife again.

"I might make you pay for it right now, Mommie

dearest!''

He held the knife under her chin, then moved it to her right breast. He lowered the sharp blade and traced an inch long scratch on the white flesh.

Alice wailed, but only a high keening came out of her bound mouth.

Gabe Young smiled. He touched the line of blood with his finger and then tasted it. His smile broadened and he used the knife again, slicing her left breast from side to side over the top, letting the blade bite into her flesh a quarter of an inch.

Blood erupted from the six inch cut.

Gabe Young laughed.

Alice's forehead beaded with sweat. She arched her back with the pain and tried to scream but the gag stopped it. She tried to roll away, but one of his strong arms pinned her belly to the bed.

"I bet you're sorry now, Mommie! Sorry you did all those dirty things to me when I was only ten years old. I couldn't even get it hard yet and you were playing with me. You didn't care, you just wanted my tongue up your pussy."

Gabe growled and sliced her right breast again so it had a half moon cut across the top. He sat back on his feet on the bed. He was still fully clothed. Only his fly hung open.

Tears melted into his eyes and dripped down. He sobbed.

"Why did you make me do all those things, Mommie? I never tried to be bad. But you said I was and I'd get a licking. You made me take down my pants and bend over your knee, but somehow you never got around to paddling me. Not when papa was gone. You knew it was bad, Mommie!"

Alice watched the knife cut her right breast and

her eyes rolled up and a low sound came from her throat as she passed out.

Gabe never noticed.

"Remember how Papa hit you that time when he caught you, and he pushed the broom handle right up between your legs? You screamed and screamed, but I think you really loved it. I don't have a broom handle, Mommie, but I have my knife. Would you like that, too?"

He spread her legs and moved the knife over her vagina and gently inserted the sharp blade. The flesh was not ready and had no chance to stretch. Blood streamed down the blade and on his hand. He roared in anger and jammed the knife up her sex slot to the hilt, then pulled it out and wiped off all the blood on the blade on her skirt still on the bed.

"Goddamned women!" He stared at the unconscious girl, then slapped her awake. "No! You are not going to faint on me again, Mommie. You did that. I threw a bucket of water on you the last time. You stay awake and watch. Everything! I am going to pay you back for everything you did to me during those four years! You just watch!"

The blade touched her skin again, drawing a blood line from her right breast down to her pubic hair. He traced another line from her left breast to the same point, but this one deeper so it bled a long dark drip line of blood.

Alice wailed through the cloth, then fainted again. Gabe never noticed.

Ten minutes later the ritual was over. Gabe was splattered with blood. Alice lay on the bed with a hundred faint blood lines on her torso, arms and legs, her face was unmarked.

Her breath came in gasps and wheezes now, but

Alice was still alive. She had not regained consciousness.

"One more lesson, Mommie. Don't ever try to rape me again. I'm a big boy now and I won't let you. If I want to play poke-poke it will be when I want to with who I want. Not you. You're too old and ugly! Just so you'll remember . . . ."

Gabe Young lifted the blade and stabbed Alice in the chest. The knife missed her heart but slid between ribs and sliced through her right breast.

He pulled the knife out and stabbed her again and again. When he got to fifty, Gabe stopped, wiped off the blade and stared down at the mutilated form on the bed. He stood, looked at the blood on his clothes, washed some of it off with water from the china bowl, then stared at the body.

He put the knife away, buttoned his fly, then wrapped Alice up in the blanket that had been under her on the bed, and carried her to the window that opened on the back alley. Without hesitation he dropped her out the window, checked the room, put on his hat and walked down the back steps to the alley.

It took him almost two hours to ride with his heavy package to the bank of the Snake River. He threw Alice and the blanket into the water and watched the swift current sweep her downstream.

A soft laugh came from Gabe.

"Nobody will ever find you, Mommie. Nobody!"

He rode back to the small town of Twin Falls, stopped at a different saloon, and drank until he could barely stand up. Then he staggered down the street on his way home. Gabe made it just inside the front door of the yellow house with the white picket fence around it before he passed out.

7

Spur McCoy found Gabe Young that afternoon in the bar where he was drinking. Spur drifted in with his hat on low and got a beer and sat at a back table and watched Young without letting him get a good look at Spur. Young was not skitterish.

Because of Young's heavy drinking, Spur decided there was little chance that the robbery could take place that evening. The next day or the next night, whichever one Young preferred. When Young took the dance hall girl upstairs to the cribs, Spur left and went back to the second room he had rented at the hotel.

The room was situated so he could see both the side and front doors to the Boise Home Bank. Damned convenient. He watched the doors until nearly midnight, then he took hour long naps and woke up precisely on the hour to check for any activity. By four A.M. he decided the robbery was to be the following day or night.

It was nearly ten A.M. before Spur got up, had

61

breakfast and walked down where he could see the small yellow painted house inside the white picket fence. There was no activity.

Just after one o'clock in the afternoon, Gabe came out blinking at the sun, and dragged himself three blocks to the hardware store. He was inside for fifteen minutes and came out with a small cardboard box and carried it home.

Spur walked into the same store and found the owner.

"Hey, Gabe Young sent me back. He said he figures he got just half enough. He didn't even tell me what it was, just said he wanted half as much more."

The owner was in his thirties, with a sharp face, long nose and bulging eyes. He frowned.

"Do tell. He must have a powerful bunch of stumps to blow out. I just sold him half a case of dynamite sticks."

"Pears he needs another quarter case then," Spur said. "He gave me plenty of money to pay for them."

Ten minutes later, Spur walked out of the store with twelve sticks of dynamite and fuse and detonator caps in a heavy paper sack. He could always use a few sticks of powder as small bombs. One thing for certain: if Gabe Young was going to use dynamite on the bank vault, it would occur when the vault was closed, at night. It would be a night hit on the Home Bank.

Spur went back to his second hotel room where he cleaned and oiled his .45 Colt and the Spencer. When both were in top shape, he gathered all his gear in his saddle bag and brought his horse around and tied her up behind the hotel.

Ten minutes before the bank was due to close at

three P.M., Spur walked in and got change for a twenty dollar gold piece. Then he asked the teller if he could use the bank's privy out back. The favor was granted, and the employee showed Spur to the door that led through the back offices. Spur thanked the clerk and held the door handle from latching and locking when it closed behind him. When he figured the clerk was back in the front of the bank, Spur pulled the back door open.

The clerk was gone. Spur found a small storage closet near the back of the bank, sat down in the corner and pulled a stack of boxes up to hide behind. Then he waited.

Five minutes later someone came to the room, took something out and left. He heard movement in the bank until nearly five o'clock, when everyone left. When he had heard no movement for ten minutes, he checked in front. The bank vault was closed and locked, the stations closed and everyone gone.

Spur checked his .45 again, as well as the hideout derringer with the two loads of birdshot. Then he settled down to wait.

When his pocket Waterbury showed that it was nine o'clock, Spur moved back to his hiding spot and waited again. He left the door to the storage room open so he could hear better.

It was just 9:30 when he heard a sledgehammer slam into the back door handle. It took only one blow, slamming the inside handle off and smashing the locking mechanism in one shot. Someone pushed the door open.

The men walked through the bank, found no one and settled down to fixing the dynamite on the vault. It was one of the old type, with a small reach-in door. Most banks would hardly call it a safe, but here it was all they had. The dynamite would be sufficient to blow it up and shatter all the windows in this end of town.

Spur had no thought of letting them set off the charge. He got out of his hiding spot and waited for one of the men to come into the back. When one did Spur clubbed him with his Colt, grabbed him as he fell and tied and gagged him. McCoy relieved him of his .44 and jammed it into his belt.

That left three.

Spur pulled out one of the three sticks of dynamite he had brought with him and fitted the fuse into the detonating cap pushed into the side of the powder. He cut the fuse to six inches and studied it. This fuse was supposed to burn a foot a minute, but the hardware man had said to allow some extra length because it had been burning faster than that.

Spur cut off two more inches of the fuse. Maybe fifteen seconds. He went to the door that led into the main part of the bank and found all three men in the vault room. That was where the vault would go if and when they got one. Spur lit the fuse from a stinker match, held it two seconds, then under-handed it through the door to the vault room.

The fuse sputtered beautifully as he threw it.

When it landed he heard a scream and one man bolted out the door. Spur tripped him, then kicked him in the side as he went down.

The blast from the one stick of powder was much less than Spur had anticipated. It did not blow out the front plate glass windows. He heard some groans from the far room. Spur crept up on the door and looked inside. One man lay draped over the bomb he was about to plant on the safe. His head had cracked open like an overripe melon where it slammed against the safe.

Gabe Young sat across the room, shaking his head, dazed and shaken by the blast.

Spur ran into the room and propelled Gabe out, took his six-gun and sat him down in a chair. He was still too confused to move.

The Secret Agent checked the front window. No one seemed concerned about the bank. The explosion had been muffled by the building.

Spur went back to Gabe, took rawhide from his pocket and tied the man's hands behind his back. Then he tied his ankles together.

By then Gabe was shaking his head, blinking.

"Dynamite . . . what the hell happened?"

"You just landed in hell, Gabe. How do you like it so far?"

Gabe squinted in the faint light. Two kerosene lamps burned as night lights to discourage robbers. Now Spur used the lamps to his advantage.

"Remember me, Gabe," Spur said, moving down close to him so he could see his face.

"Hell no. What blew up?"

"Not your big bomb, just one stick I sent in for your inspection."

"Who the hell are you?"

"I thought you might remember. Four days ago, down by Twin Falls, you were in a posse. You lynched somebody."

"Yeah, so?"

"You hung me, you bastard!"

"Not a chance, that guy was dead."

"Guess again, bastard. It was a trick knot the sheriff tied for you."

Gabe stared at him, then laughed without humor. "Hell, yes. I remember your ugly face. Sure as hell should have used you for target practice as well as hanging you."

"Is that your reaction? You lynch an innocent man and all you can say is you should have shot him, too?"

"That's enough. Because Will is gonna blast you about now!"

Spur dropped and rolled to the side. He heard the shot just after he moved. It missed. His Colt came up stuttering hot lead. Two rounds cut through the man called Will who stood in the doorway to the back room. One sliced into his heart, the other caught him just under the chin and splattered half his head against the wall.

Spur rolled to his feet and ran to the back room. The first man he had tied was still there.

"Your games are over, Gabe. This one is not only for me, it's for the women you've hurt over the years. Like that sixteen year old on the ranch just out of Twin Falls where you stayed the night.

"Hell, she wanted . . ."

Spur slammed his fist into Gabe's mouth choking off the words. The man jolted off the chair to the floor.

McCoy opened his shirt and unwound a twenty foot length of half inch rope he had wrapped around his body. He slowly, methodically, tied a hangman's noose in one end.

"This is the way it's done, Young. You can show all your buddies in hell how to do it."

"What the hell?"

"You're going to hang, Young. You're going to have the pleasure of thinking about dying, then the rapture of feeling that rope tighten around your neck and strangling you for a few seconds before your neck breaks as you hit the bottom of the rope.

"You'll never hang another man, Young. You're a dead man. Any more jokes?"

Young wouldn't talk after that. Spur found an overhead beam in the bank and threw the rope over it. He pushed over a desk and a small table and lifted Young up until he stood on the top one. Spur put Young's head into the noose, then tightened the slack and snugged the knot up to the outlaw's right side of his chin.

"Any last words, killer?" Spur asked.

Young glared at him. Shook his head.

"The short, dirty life of Gabe Young."

Young snorted. "Get on with it."

Spur knew he should take the man to the sheriff, let justice take its course. He was supposed to be supporting, upholding, defending, making the system of criminal laws work.

Damnit, not this time! Not until his neck was healed. He'd turned too many killers over to judges and juries and seen them walk out of prison two or three years later. Then he had to do the whole job over again when another innocent man fell at the hands of the ex-convicts.

Not this time!

Goddamnit, not this time!

With a vicious jolt from his shoulder, he powered the desk and small table backward.

Gabe Young fell off the table, plummeted two feet down, then hit the bottom of the rope and the knots held.

Spur heard a crack, like the breaking of an inch thick stick of wood. He looked up and saw Gabe's neck slanted to the side at an unnatural angle. His neck was broken.

Gabe's feet twitched. Spur looked in surprise at how long the man's involuntary muscles kept trying to function, even after his heart had stopped beating and his lungs stopped pumping oxygen.

Spur looked at Gabe's face. His eyes bulged out, and his tongue lolled out of his mouth.

Rest In Peace?

Absolutely not! "Burn in Hell, you bastard!" Spur McCoy thought as he checked the dead man by the back room door, then the live one and slipped out the back door. The bank employees would find a grisly mess in the morning, but at least their bank was safe, and Gabe Young was burning in hell.

Spur closed the door of the bank and walked two blocks to the hotel. His horse was ready and waiting where he had left her. He mounted and rode out. This time there would be no problem. He would ride to the first stagecoach stop about ten miles out of Boise and buy a ticket to Twin Falls. He still had two more men to track down so he could make sure that justice was done. He would make sure, because he would be judge, jury and executioner!

8

During the four days and nights of the stage ride back to Twin Falls, Spur McCoy had plenty of time to consider his situation.

He had been on his way to Twin Falls to investigate a case of counterfeiting when he wound up on the end of that rope. Someone was turning out nearly perfect twenty dollar bills. The dead give-away was that each bill had the same serious number. Only a dozen or so had been turned in, mostly by banks that caught the serial number. The Twin Falls bank had taken the loss rather than arouse the whole community. Some of the bills had been spotted in Boise.

Most of them, however, had surfaced in Twin Falls, and that was the place where Spur was to make his contact.

He had only a name, Van Buren, man or woman he didn't know. He was to meet the person after he registered at the Pocatello hotel under his real name. This was his first trip to Idaho so there

69

shouldn't be many people who knew him or what he did.

Spur had pushed all this into the background with the killing surge that filled him after his lynching. He was still a haunted man, still blood lusting for the corpses of the other two men who hung him. He shivered just remembering what he felt when that horse surged out from under him and he sensed the rope tightening as he fell toward the end of the slack . . .

He looked out the window and shuddered remembering. It was over. He had to forget. But he couldn't forget, he never would. Spur took a deep breath and smiled at the woman across from him in the big Concord stagecoach. There were only three passengers. The third was a drummer, a salesman for something. He hadn't tried to push his wares and Spur was just as happy. His leg and neck both began to hurt the second day. The third day he bought a bottle of whiskey from the man who ran the coach stop and provided them beds and food.

The last two days into Twin Falls Spur spent in a soft alcoholic glow, but it killed the pain so he stopped groaning.

All the time he kept reminding himself he had to work on the counterfeiting. He knew where the other two hangmen were. He could get them anytime. All he had to do was make sure that the merchant, Josh Hoffer, didn't recognize him before Spur was ready.

When the stage rolled in, Spur talked the driver into letting him off at Doc Rawson's little home office. He did and Spur grabbed his saddlebags, untied the lead rope on his horse and limped into the medic's office.

A pregnant woman sat in the waiting room. She blushed the moment Spur came in and turned toward the wall. Most women hid their pregnancies in public as long as they could. Then they stayed home for the last few months.

When Doc got to Spur he snorted and swore for a minute.

"Damn fool, you could be dead by now. You didn't help your leg any. You want me to have to cut it off at the knee?"

That got Spur's attention. "Fix it, Doc. I got business."

"Bet you have. The undertaker can always use another two dollars. Christ! Why won't you people understand how serious something like this can be?"

"I been on a stage for four days."

"Good. Now I want you to stay off the leg for at least two more days. Get a hotel room and sleep. Here." He held out a glass of water he had mixed with two teaspoons of medicine.

"Drink this, and I'll be back and change the bandages."

Spur had the medicine drained before he realized what it was. Laudanum. A tincture of opium. In an hour he wouldn't care who he was or where he was. Already he could feel the pain receding and his head becoming light. Hell, so he'd take off two days and eat and sleep.

When Doc Rawson came back a half hour later, Spur hardly reacted when he pulled the stuck on bandages off his neck. The wound had healed little in the six days. It should be farther along. The medic put on more salve and bandaged it. At least there were no ugly red lines of infection.

By the time Doc was finished Spur could hardly walk. The sawbones closed his office and brought around his buggy.

Ten minutes later he had Spur deposited on a bed in a room on the first floor of the Pocatello hotel. Doc registered him as Harry Smith and paid for two nights lodging from Spur's new wallet. Doc was surprised at the amount of cash Spur carried.

"See that he gets two meals a day brought to his room," Doc told the room clerk. "I'll be past once a day to check on him and give him more medicine."

When the doctor left, a small, dark haired woman talked to the clerk.

"Has Mr. McCoy checked in yet?" she asked.

"Not recently, Ma'am," the clerk said. "You can look at the register if you want to."

"No, that won't be necessary." She frowned, then lifted arched brows. "I'll be back after the stage comes in tomorrow."

Two days later, Spur woke up in the morning with a bad taste in his mouth, a pounding headache and feeling as though he had been wading through a sewer.

He got up and dressed in city clothes, shaved off what looked like three days growth of beard, and made his way slowly down to the dining room. There wasn't enough breakfast in the place for him. He had two orders of eggs, bacon and flapjacks, two big cups of coffee and a helping of canned peaches.

The food killed his headache and made him feel partly human.

The Laudanum! Doc put him on it to keep him corralled! The stuff could get to be a habit. He'd seen it happen before, start out as medicine and soon the victim graduated into pure opium.

At the desk he asked if there were any messages for Spur McCoy, and the clerk lifted his brows.

"You've been registered under another name, here it is, Harry Smith."

"Good name. I've known lots of Harry Smiths. Change it to Spur McCoy and I'll pay you for three more nights."

"Someone has been asking for you," the clerk said.

"Good. Next time tell the person I'm here."

Spur was still a little shaky. His leg felt better, but he had trouble turning his head. He went to Doc Rawson's office to thank him, and see if the bandage needed changing. It did.

Back at the hotel the clerk signalled to him and handed him an envelope. Inside the feminine hand asked him to meet her in front of the bakery at 9:30 A.M. She would be in a black, closed buggy.

Spur checked the hotel's Seth Thomas. It was nearly that time now. He walked the two blocks to the bakery, and found the exercise made both his leg and neck feel better. He saw the black closed buggy and walked up to it. The store side door opened and he pulled it wider and looked in.

A small, attractive woman with dark hair nodded at him.

"Please get in quickly. I can't be seen with you."

He stepped in and she drove the rig down the street and into the residential area three blocks away.

"Mr. McCoy. My name is Mrs. Kane Turner. Eugenia Turner. I contacted the government some time ago. I assume you're here about the counterfeiting?"

He held out his hand. "Yes, Ma'am. I am McCoy,

Secret Service Agent working with the United States Treasury. Counterfeiting is one of our major responsibilities. The director asked me to thank you for your concern."

"I'm more worried about my husband than the general economy of the country, Mr. McCoy. I'm afraid he is mixed up with some unsavory characters here in town, and that they are counterfeiting twenty dollar bills. He has been spending a lot of evenings downtown lately. Once I deliberately followed him and he went to the newspaper office of all places."

"Mrs. Turner. You realize this could get your husband in a lot of trouble. If he is counterfeiting it could mean he would have to go to prison for at least ten years."

"Yes, I know." She looked up him with big brown eyes. For a moment they were troubled. "I would rather give him up for ten years than have him killed. I think he is in real danger with these men."

She reached in her reticule and took out an envelope.

"Look inside, Mr. McCoy."

He did and found three twenty dollar bills. When he spread them out he found that each had the same serial number.

"Counterfeit," he said.

"Yes. At home Mr. Turner hid a box of them. I counted them one day. Each stack has a hundred in it, and there are fifty stacks. That's a hundred thousand dollars!"

"And all worthless, Mrs. Turner."

"Unless he spends it, passes it." Tears seeped out of her eyes. She brushed them away. She looked so small and so hurt and so alone, that Spur wanted to reach over and take her in his arms and comfort her. He touched her shoulder and she swayed toward him a moment, then moved back.

"Mr. McCoy, I have thought a lot about this. I am not used to dealing with tragedy or lawbreaking. I don't know if I should have told you this or not."

"Yes, you did the right thing. Even though he is your husband, he is breaking the law. Thousands of people could be hurt by what he is doing. I'm tremendously impressed by what you have done, and proud of you, Eugenia Turner."

She looked up and tried to smile. "Mr. McCoy, thank you. It's good to know that someone agrees with me. If I hear anything or if I can help you, I'll contact you by leaving a message in your box at the hotel. Now I better take you back to town so I can get back home."

"Thanks for what you're doing, Mrs. Turner. What you are doing is the right thing, believe me."

She let him off near the hotel, then drove away. He walked at once to the small office of the newspaper, THE TWIN FALLS GAZETTE, and went inside.

The familiar smell came at once: the musty slightly sulphur scent of the stacks of newsprint mixed with the acid black smell of the printer's ink. It was an odor Spur would never forget, and one you could find nowhere but in a newspaper office.

A small, thin man with a green visor and wearing eye glasses looked up from a desk behind a waist high counter that ran across the width of the room.

"Yes? You're new in town. Doc was treating you for a bad leg and a neck injury."

Spur chuckled. "Never try to keep anything from a news man. I also am in the trade, or rather nearly. I arrange the sale of newspapers, my speciality. And right now I have a buyer for your paper, your plant, your circulation, advertisers and of course for your good will.''

"Hadn't thought of selling. Doing very nicely here now. Town is growing. I expect to be the biggest city in Idaho by the time we get statehood. In the best spot for it. Pocatello will grow and so will Boise because it's the capital, but Twin Falls! We have everything right here!''

"This is known as driving up the price. My name is Spur McCoy, of St. Louis.''

The small man stood. He wore a black suit with vest and a string black tie. He held out his hand across the counter.

"Good to meet you. I'm H. Larson Wintergarden, publisher, editor, accountant, pressman, circulation, janitor and general handyman.''

"Sounds like a big staff. Understand you have some good equipment. Could I buy the two-bit tour?''

A half hour later Spur knew more about the small plant than he needed to. The important part was the press. This one horse newspaper had one of the best presses made. It was an Issac Adams bed-and-platen press for job work. It had an iron frame, not wooden, with a fixed platen immovably set in the frame. The form was put on an iron bed and this bed raised against the fixed platen. Spur was no expert in presses, but he knew the Issac Adams. The press figured in over two thirds of counterfeiting done on paper currency in the U.S.

He had listened to the merits of the press when Wintergarden extrolled them, but sluffed them off, pretending he was more interested in the flat bed newsprint press.

After the tour, the newsman sat in his chair, and lit a large, fat cigar.

"I'm not really interested in selling, Mr. McCoy, but say I was. What kind of an offer would you make?"

"My standard offer, twice your last year's gross. A flat $3,000."

Wintergarden laughed.

"That is for the newspaper," Spur hurried on. "I don't want your expensive Adams. Why in the world did you get such a high priced press for a small town like this? There is no way that you can make enough to pay for it in five years here in Twin Falls."

Wintergarden hedged. He flicked off the ashes and tried to pass it off.

"Oh, the Adams. Sure, she's a fine press, but I do a big business in job work. Get some in from Pocatello on the stage. I plan on going in heavily into job printing, so I had a chance to pick up this Adams for a song. Printer went bankrupt and I got it for ten cents on the dollar."

"Well, no matter," Spur said. "I still wouldn't need it. You think over my offer. I'll be around another few days until Doc says I can travel. You let me know. I'll be at the Pocatello Hotel."

"I'll do that. Right nice of you to stop by."

Spur went out the front door into the still morning sunshine. The press was the best ever made for precise job work, especially when paper went through the press the second time to put on the second color. He was making progress quicker than he figured. The lawyer and the printer. Who else did they need? Mrs. Turner had said "those men", so there must be more.

It was time to check in with the sheriff.

Sheriff Abraham Lincoln Sloan smiled when he saw Spur limp into his office.

"McCoy. Wondered where you went. You look worse now than when I dropped you off at Doc Rawson's a week ago."

"Feel a mite worse, too. We need to have a confidential talk. You have a few minutes?"

Sheriff Sloan led Spur into his office that had a door, and closed it.

"Sheriff Sloan, I'm here on a counterfeiting problem. We've found twenty dollar bills circulating that are worthless. All signs point to them coming from here in Twin Falls . . ."

"Damn. I was hoping they were just passed here by somebody from Boise or Cheyenne or Denver. What can I do?"

"Keep it quiet for now, and tell me what you know about H. Lawson Wintergarden, printer."

"Figures. He came to town two years ago, started the newspaper from scratch. Worked damn hard. First week he was here he came in and told me that he had been in some trouble back east, but he paid the price and he was free and clear of any legal problems. He just wanted to get it off his chest, I think. He also said then if anybody tried to blackmail him, they wouldn't be able to."

"Given you any trouble since?"

"None. I work with him so he can report arrests and court cases. It's been coming out just fine."

Spur told him about the expensive job press and how they had been used before for counterfeiting.

"Damn, you got any more bills?"

Spur showed him the three Mrs. Turner had given him.

"That ties it! What we going to do?"

"I just wanted to know the background on the printer. There have to be more people involved. Finding them is my job."

"Let me know if I can help." The sheriff stood and walked to the case holding six rifles. He picked one up and then put it back.

"Oh, got a flyer in yesterday from Boise. Seems they had a bank robbery. At least an attempted bank robbery. Went bad for the robbers. One of them got shot dead, a second one knocked out and tied up. Third one got smashed up by a dynamite blast in the vault room. The fourth one was hanged to a beam right there in the bank. Seem strange to you, McCoy?"

"Must have been some vigilante group that caught them," Spur said.

"Must have been. The guy who was hanged was your old necktie party friend, Gabe Young."

"Well, what do you know about that! Looks like I won't have to track him down then, don't it?"

"Looks that way." The sheriff paused. "Not my jurisdiction, of course. But I would hope that you could prove you were here in Twin Falls that day Young was hanged, if you ever had to."

"Like you said, Sheriff, it isn't your jurisdiction."

"Mmmmmm. Thought you might say something like that. Do I need to warn you about the other two, Hoffer and Dallman? There wasn't any charges I could bring against them. Now if you had died correct and proper, I could have . . ."

"Could have . . . yeah," Spur said. "As for me, I got some counterfeiters to worry about. Oh, did Wintergarden say where he was from? What state, what town? Like to know what he served time for if it's possible. Also if Wintergarden is his real name."

"No way I can find out, unless I ask him."

"Yeah, figured. Thanks for the help, Sheriff, and for telling me about Young. Man was on the road to hell for a long time. His luck finally ran out."

9

Spur McCoy went to the livery stable from the sheriff's office. He saddled his mare and got directions to the Boots Dallman homestead. It was only about five miles out of town.

On the way Spur decided he should find out more about Dallman. Right now he was riding blind after the man. He wanted to know what made the man function.

The place was a typical homestead, 160 acres of land that held part of a valley and some hills to the south. The frame house was small but could be expanded with each child if necessary. As he rode down the lane from a scratch trail, Spur saw about thirty cattle grazing behind barbed wire. Beyond them was a plowed field and a second field of wheat growing emerald green on the near side. Farming and cattle. It never had worked yet.

Spur rode up to the brown painted house with white trim and tied his mount at the hitching rail.

The screen door banged and a woman stood just

outside of the house thirty feet away. She carried a single barreled shotgun and watched him.

"Far enough," she said.

"Afternoon, Mrs. Dallman. I was hoping to find Boots at home, but seeings as how you have the scattergun, I'd say he isn't here. Right?"

"Right. What do you want with Boots?"

"Just a small matter we need to talk about. I've got some of the new British beef cattle breeding stock, and I thought he might like to take a look at them."

The shotgun lowered a few inches.

"Boots is working at the Box B. Won't be home until after supper time. They doing a roundup over there for a week or so more."

"When does he get time to do all the work around here?"

"We manage. I do lots of it."

"Your name is Martha?" Spur asked.

"Yes. You didn't say your name."

"Bainbridge, the B Bar B. About twenty miles upstream. Came into town so I took the chance I could find him."

"Sorry I can't invite you in. Boots don't hold with any visitors when he isn't here. Too many renegades and rawhiders around again." The shotgun now aimed at the ground.

From twenty feet away he could see that Martha Dallman was about twenty-five, still pretty, not yet ground down by the hard work and unrelenting toll of the elements on a farm. She had a good figure and was tall for a woman, five feet six maybe.

She put the shotgun over her shoulder and shrugged.

"Sorry about the silly gun. Boots says I got to. I

did scare off some wild grubstake rider one day who
decided he could take what he wanted."

"Pays to be careful, even in these days. You tell
Boots I was by, Bainbridge. I'll try and see him next
time I'm in town or I'll write him a letter. You pick
up mail in town?"

"Sure, at the Mercantile. He's the postmaster."

"Fine, Mrs. Dallman. It's been pleasant talking to
you. Hope to see you and Boots again one of these
days."

He mounted up, tipped his hat and walked the
mare back down the lane. As he left he surveyed the
house, the barn, a corncrib and big chicken house.
There was a hog pen at the rear of the barn.

Boots Dallman had the look of a farmer. Everything was neat, tools put away, the buildings in
good repair, and the house painted.

This was no fly-by-night drunk who charged into a
lynching. He even gave his pretty wife instructions
about the use of a shotgun and how to handle
strangers. Boots Dallman did not fit into the usual
pattern of a wild-eyed, hell-bent anything-for-fun
lynching participant.

As Spur rode back to town, he tried to remember
what Boots did in the lynching. He did not know or
would not tie the hangman's knot. Boots was not
one of the pair who jabbed the mare to surge her out
from under Spur. The man had been there, in the
background. But he had not spoken out, he had not
opposed the lynching.

When the sheriff talked to him that day, he had
said something about Boots being drunk, still
drunk. That he had been drunk for two days?
Possible. Still he had been a participant. Again Spur
felt the overwhelming panic and agony as the rope

tightened around his neck and he knew he was about
to enter eternity. No! All three had to hang!

Back at the livery he asked the swamper what
store Josh ran.

"Got to be Josh Hoffer. He runs the Hoffer Mercantile, just across from the bank." Spur thanked
him and walked down to the bank corner.

The Mercantile was the biggest and looked like
the best store in town. It boasted of having
anything you wanted. "Better stock than any store
in Boise!"

To Spur, that sounded like a good way to go
broke. Maybe Hoffer was independently wealthy
and just used the store as a hobby.

Spur made sure his blue neckerchief covered the
bandage on his throat, then he pulled his low
crowned brown hat down over his eyes and walked
into the store. He moved away from the counter and
watched the man wrapping up someone's purchase.

It was Hoffer all right, short and dumpy and
wheezing as he walked. There were three or four
others in the store, so Hoffer was busy with them.
The store was interesting. It had a lot of
merchandise that Spur might expect to see in St.
Louis or Chicago stores, but not in the wilds of
Idaho. How could Hoffer afford to keep a stock like
this, including fancy china and leaded glass?

The store had hardware and software, and
women's wear all in one. He had a full line of
groceries, tools, farm equipment, even rolls of
barbed wire, which the cattlemen hated and the
farmers said was the only way they could keep them
roaming cattle from eating up their crops.

Spur made sure Hoffer did not see his face. He
studied the place for five minutes, then slipped out

the front door. There was no hurry about Hoffer.
His part in the hanging would forever be sharp and
clear. He wasn't the idea man, but he came through
as a follower who enjoyed watching a man stretch a
rope. There was no rush taking care of Hoffer. At
least Spur knew he had touched all three bases now.
He could concentrate for a day or two on the
counterfeit problem.

Spur got to the bank just before it closed. He
asked to see the bank president and showed him a
twenty dollar bill, one of the counterfeits. The bank
man was in his fifties, balding, with eyeglasses that
perched on his nose without earpieces.

"Someone told me this bill was no good," Spur
said. "Looks good to me. What do you think?"

The bank man looked at it a moment.

"It's genuine. I can spot a bad bill by the feel of
the paper. This one is fine. I'll be glad to give you
change for it if you like." Spur almost let him, serve
the pompous bastard right. But Spur put the bill
back in his wallet.

"No, no. I like to have one big bill with me. Takes
up less room than all those ones and fives. Thank
you, sir." Spur left the bank with his question still
unanswered. There were three banks in the little
town. Was this one a part of the conspiracy? On the
other hand, maybe the bank president really didn't
know real money from the good counterfeit. It was a
problem Spur was going to have to solve before
long.

It was near quitting time when Spur walked past
the printing office and newspaper. There appeared
to be no one there. A note on the door explained.

"Town Council meeting tonight. I'll be there if
anyone has any important business that must be

transacted." It was signed H. L. Wintergarden. Spur watched the place from beside a friendly maple tree up the street. An hour later he gave up. No one had come or gone from the front or the side door of the newspaper and printing plant. If any more fake money was going to be printed it was not going to be tonight. Spur guessed that no one in town except Wintergarden could possibly run the printing press.

Spur decided to wash up before he went to the Pocatello Hotel dining room. He came to his hotel room on the first floor and used his key and stepped inside. For a moment he thought he was in the wrong room.

A woman stood before the dresser mirror combing her long, dark hair.

"Good, I hoped you would come soon," she said. When she turned he saw that she was Eugenia Turner, wife of the lawyer.

She put down the comb and smiled at him. He had not seen her standing before. She was barely five feet and an inch tall. Her wide set brown eyes smiled at him.

"You wonder how I got in. I stood in the hall and people kept staring at me, so I simply used one of the keys from my home. These old door locks are not very good. There are only two basic types, so here I am. I hope you don't mind."

Spur took off his hat and dropped it on the bed.

"Not at all. The fact is, I wanted to talk to you. Do you think any of the bankers know about these bills?"

She frowned slightly, then slowly shook her head. "One of them might, Al Jones is extremely smart and quick. He could have spotted them if more than one came to his attention. The other two are not really bankers, just men who had some money and decided they would open banks."

She turned and her hair flowed with her in a black swirl.

"Kane went downtown tonight again. I almost wish he were going to see a woman, but I know it isn't that. Were they working at the printing office?"

"No, I checked it before I came here. There's a city council meeting or something like that."

"Oh, yes, that's right. Kane goes to those, too. I was hoping you might have caught Kane printing money."

"Do you want me to open the door? I mean it isn't quite proper for you here, in my room and all . . ."

"I really don't think you need to worry about that." She walked toward him, smiling. Her dress was tight, showing her breasts, her small tight waist and the flare of her hips before the material fell to the floor.

"I've never been one to worry to much about conventions, and idle talk." She watched him, then let her obvious stare wander deliciously down his body. She paused at his crotch, looked back at him quickly and smiled.

"You certainly are a big man. I've always liked big men. They seem so sure of themselves, so in control. Perhaps sometimes we could . . . " She broke it off and walked to the window.

"Mr. McCoy, I lied to you the other day. I hope that my husband gets caught. I'll do all I can to help you. He's guilty. The fact is I don't like my husband very much. He lied to me before we were married. He has lied to me consistently since. He married me for my money and no other reason."

She lifted her chin and stared at him. "Does my telling you this surprise you, Mr. McCoy?"

"I am surprised by very little these days, Mrs. Turner."

"Then maybe I can shock you. Kane Turner has not slept in my bed for six months. He has not made love to me for almost a year. Does that shock you?"

"No, but it does surprise me. You are an extremely beautiful woman."

She walked to him, reached up to be kissed and Spur bent and kissed her partly open mouth. She pushed hard against him, her whole body melting against his.

She held the kiss a long time, then broke it off slowly. She pushed back from him, caught his hand and held it over her breast. She said nothing more. Her eyes were closed as she felt his hand massage her breast tenderly.

Eugenia sighed softly, opened her eyes and pulled up his hand and kissed it.

"Mr. McCoy, perhaps sometime . . . I mean when you're not busy, I might come back here and . . ." She sighed again, caught up a reticule from the dresser and stood in the soft lamplight.

Spur put his hand on the doorknob and bent, kissing her on the cheek.

"Mrs. Turner, you are a delightful person, and I'm always ready to help comfort you in any way I can."

She smiled, reached up and kissed his lips. She came away slowly. "I hope we can figure out some way you can comfort me, Mr. McCoy." She stopped and looked at him. "You have the most wonderful smile!" She reached in and kissed his shirt over his chest, opened the door and went out without looking back.

10

Josh Hoffer closed his store and stared around. Damn but it was a great little store! He had items here you would have to go at least all the way to Denver or Frisco to find! Yeah, and he was going to have more!

He paid no attention to his wife nagging him about the stock. She said he had houseware items that would not sell in New York City to the rich folks. He was wasting money. But he could not resist a fine piece of china, or delicate glasswork. He was an artist and always would be, despite his current role of playing the bumpkin mercantile owner. A man had to reach out and grasp what he could, but his dreams were there and no one had a right to interfere with them.

His left hand rubbed the mole on his left cheek without his realizing it. The habit had become ingrained lately.

For just a minute Hoffer thought of all the money he had in that cardboard box under the floorboards behind the counter.

"Three hundred thousand fucking dollars!" Hoffer said it aloud, softly almost with reverence. Money was tremendously important to him. Money opened the whole wide world to a person. You could do what you wanted, travel where you wanted to go, have all the best of the fancy women, buy the finest whiskey and food anywhere in the world!

Hoffer wiped a bead of sweat off his forehead. He always sweat when he thought what he was going to do with his money. If it all had been passed and *changed* he would make up his mind in a second.

Yes, the store would go. He would sell out for what he could get and travel. He was almost certain of that. He would simply vanish one day, leaving a few debts and his wife in the house on the side street!

Hoffer chuckled. What a surprise that would be for that old woman! Then he could find some sweet young thing about sixteen and teach her what he wanted her to know . . . and how to fuck the way he liked. Oh yeah!

Hoffer checked his watch. It was two minutes after six. He went to the alley door of his store and lifted the bar he had across the door. At once it came open and Kane Turner stood there.

"I don't like to be kept waiting, Hoffer, not by anybody."

Hoffer shivered in anger. His lips went white and he folded his arms, as his face turned red.

"You high falluting bastard! Don't get prissy and nasty with me or I'll cut you off at the pockets. Never did like you. I have to work with you but I sure as shit don't have to LIKE you!"

"Easy, easy old man, you'll have an attack,"

Turner said. He slipped in the door and pushed the bar back in place. "Sorry, I didn't mean to get you riled up. Just thinking about this money makes me edgy. You said you had a plan to pass a lot of it."

"True." Hoffer took a deep breath. His face began returning to normal and he rubbed the mole. "Yeah, I got a plan. Didn't mean to blow up that way."

"Where is it?"

"Put away."

"Don't you take it out and look at it? I leaf through those stacks almost every night! All that money is fascinating, even if it is phony."

"I know it's safe, that's enough for me right now," Hoffer said. "Come into my office."

They went across the storage area of the store to a small office that had been built into the side of the big room. It had a rolltop desk, a dozen big boxes and two chairs. Hoffer took out a bottle of whiskey and splashed two fingers into two water glasses. He sipped his, and put it down.

Hoffer looked up at Turner. Even sitting down he had to look up at the bastard! He was tall, over five feet ten, and wore a suit of gray wool that must be hot, but he never had seen Turner sweat.

Josh scrubbed one hand back over his thinning brown hair and stared at Turner through slitted, close set green eyes.

"San Francisco," he said.

"What?" Turner asked. "What about San Francisco?"

"That's where we pass the money. We take our *used* bills out there and pass them at the stores, getting at least fifteen dollars change for anything we buy."

"That will take lots of time and we only make

seventy-five percent of the face value."

Hoffer laughed. "You're new to this game, aren't you, Turner? Any counterfeiter worth his plates knows that if he can get fifteen to twenty percent of the face value he's a rich man. The only problem here is the slowness and the exposure. We could work maybe three or four days, then we'd have to leave because by that time the phony bills would get to the banks and somebody would spot the counterfeiting. The secret is to buy something for a dollar or two, use a twenty, then pocket the change and throw away the item. Even haggle over the price."

"We might pass twenty-five bills a day that way," Turner said. "That's only five hundred dollars a day, and if we made seventy-five percent that would only be something over four hundred dollars a day."

"That's the average wage for a working man these days for all year, Turner. How much did you make last year as a lawyer?"

"Yes, I see your point. But four days would be a thousand and five hundred, maybe. Then we would have to leave. Isn't there a better way?"

"Not for immediate cash."

"How about buying a big item like a house in San Francisco, pay say a thousand dollars for it with bogus money. Then sell it to someone else and get real money!"

"That is ridiculously stupid, Turner! You're supposed to be a lawyer! Buying a house in San Francisco would take legal signatures, identification. And the first time the banker looked at those new twenties with the same serial numbers you'd be in a federal prison for twenty years."

"Is the way we're doing it here any better, any safer?"

"With these hicks and these dumb as grass bankers, it really doesn't matter. The bills are almost perfect. I'm at artist, I tell you! Not even the banker flicked an eye when I gave him a twenty last week. He snapped it once and gave me a double eagle. I told him I needed a pocket piece!"

"Josh took out a basket and put it beside him. From the desk drawer he pulled out a packet of a hundred twenty-dollar bills and began crumpling them up one at a time and dropping them in the basket.

"What the hell are you doing?" Turner asked.

"Not even a banker will question a couple of used twenty-dollar bills. These are going to look well used when I get through with them. First I crumple them up, then I sprinkle some dust and sand over them and mix them up. A few sprays of fine water mist and then I stir them again. By the time they dry and I take them out and smooth them into a stack again, it will be two inches high instead of an inch."

"I'll have to do that with some of mine."

"Turner, remember, don't pass more than two a week."

Josh took four of the new bills and put them in his wallet between good bills, then put the wallet back in his pocket.

"They pick up the smell of leather that way, and the other bills," Josh said. "Anything that works."

"You seen that new man in town?" Turner asked. "He's been sniffing around. I saw him come out of the print shop."

"Haven't noticed anybody."

"He's big, over six feet, looks like he could be mean as hell if he got pushed around."

"We can't worry about every stranger in town."

Turner sighed. "Yeah, guess you're right. I am more concerned about our real estate campaign. How long can we convince these people to keep the counterfeit cash out of the banks?"

"You're the lawyer, you figure it out," Josh said. "I can't do every damn thing in this operation. Christ! I got together with Wintergarden and we brought in the damn press. I've done damn near everything."

"Easy, Josh, just settle down. We can work it all out. So far I've bought six buildings on my side of the street. I gave them a hundred dollars down, all partly *used* bills the way you fixed them. The rest of it is on promissory notes on each parcel, set up on yearly payments, one fourth each year for the next four years."

Josh tipped the glass of sipping whiskey again, pursed his lips and looked over at his visitor. "That's about the way you figured it would work. What's the problem? We process enough of the fake bills so we can pay in real money each of the payments. No bank problems." Josh hiccuped and took another shot of whiskey.

"I've bought five properties along on this side. I set mine up on monthly payments, for two years. So I need to launder just enough of the fake bills each month to make the payments. No big bundle of the bogus money goes to the bank this way. Even so, the Federal people are going to get a report of the funny money before long. So we have to be pristine pure by that time."

"In another three months we will own the whole damn town!" Turner said. He slicked back heavy black hair and chuckled. "Right now we buy the business, then rent the building back to the merchant. When we have most of the town, we'll charge any rent we want to, or close up the firms there and open our own. We can even change the name of the town if we want to. Turnerville might be nice!''

Josh kept wadding up the twenty dollar bills and dropping them in the basket.

"You still in line to be mayor in the election next week?"

"Absolutely. And I am prepared to represent my constituents to the best of my ability."

"Bullshit?" Josh said and they both laughed. "You represent our own interests or I'll have you thrown out of office." Both men laughed again and the atmopshere eased.

"So we have the city council in our pocket," Turner said. "You'll be elected again next year, and we can outvote anyone they put up against us around here."

Josh finished crumpling the bills. Now he stirred them around, sprinkled on sand and dust, then sprinkled drips of water on them from his hand. He put the basket to one side to let the bills dry.

"How in hell did you recognize Wintergarden," Turner asked.

"Wasn't hard. I spent almost two years with him back in Illinois where we both worked for the state. His term was up a year before mine so I figured I'd never see him again. Printers and plate makers always kind of get together in prison, just to outbrag each other if nothing else. He had heard of my work in Chicago. I knew he was a top pressman, so we figured if we ever got out we might work together."

"Then you lost track of him?"

"Until he came in to town here to run the newspaper. It's a cover-up he's used before. But he had changed his looks. He used to be chunky, real chubby. And he never wore glasses before, and he always wore his black hair full, almost Indian long. Now he's a blond, with a short, short haircut, and thin as a pine tree. I don't know how he does it."

"But he didn't jump at your offer?"

"Not right away. Denied who he was. He had changed his name, too. But I tricked him into admitting his past. From then on it was easy. He needed the money to prop up his little stinking newspaper. We sure as shit won't get any bad publicity in his paper about the city council, or what we do!"

"And he gets enough money on the side to keep his little paper operating," Turner said. He stared at Hoffer who had begun straightening out the money.

"You wad up two thousand dollars every night?" Turner asked.

"Only on good nights," Hoffer said. He pointed a finger at Turner and his voice dropped into a serious tone. "You keep that wife of yours under control. We don't want her finding that money and going on a buying tear in the stores."

"Don't worry. She's trying to get pregnant. Right now that takes up most of her time." He grinned. "That's why I'm so worn out these days."

"Keep her barefoot, in a nightgown and pregnant, and you won't have any trouble with her." Josh put the two thousand dollars back in the bottom drawer, locked it and stood.

"Now I've got to get home. I'm hungry as hell and I know I'm going to have steak tonight."

They went out the back door, said goodbye and

Hoffer watched the lawyer walk out the long way along the alley.

He never really liked that son of a bitch, but Hoffer knew they needed him, at least for another few months. Then Kane Turner was going to have a serious, and undoubtedly a fatal accident!

11

When Spur woke up the next morning, he had changed his mind. The more he thought about Boots Dallman's wife, Martha, the more worried he became. She would tell Boots about him. She was that kind of woman who would do what her man told her, and fight like hell to protect him. She had been afraid of Spur, he sensed that.

Dallman would know there were no ranchers in the area with new English breeding stock. She would desribe Spur right down to the neckerchief around his throat and Dallman would be off and running.

His only hope was that Dallman had worked so late the night before he couldn't ride home. Or, if he got home he was so tired he did not connect the stranger at his ranch with the man he tried to hang.

Either way it was a poor gamble.

Spur had breakfast as soon as the dining room opened at six A.M. and rode for the Box B ranch which he found out was only three miles from town, but the opposite way from Dallman's. It was worth a try.

For two miles he rode along a dirt road that had barbed wire fences on both sides. The fences protected field crops from the wandering beef cattle, which still dominated this section of the land around Twin Falls. That was despite the long drive it took every summer to get them to a railroad siding where they could be loaded for shipment east.

Spur found a ranch hand just inside the big gate of the Box B.

"Hell, they never come back last night. Up in the breaks there to the south about five miles out, I'd say. Been branding young stuff and castrating the young bulls into steers."

"Is Boots with them?"

"Hell, yes. He's one of our top ropers. He's an expert at getting that loop around a steer's back two feet for a two horse catch."

Spur got directions and rode south. Before long he saw burned out campfires where the crew had worked at branding and gathering the herd. Then two miles off he saw three cowboys sashaying a dozen cattle toward a small valley. He got there about the same time the critters did.

A man left the trio of horsemen and rode to meet Spur. The man sat tall in the saddle, ramrod holding up his spine, and it spoke of a total military background. Cavalry no doubt.

The man was in his forties, tanned, wore a moustache and had blue eyes that squinted in perpetual defense against the bright sun. His hands were large and looked able. He rode with his right hand hanging at his side near a six-gun that leathered there.

"Morning," the stranger said.

"Yes, good morning. I'm looking for an old friend of mine, Boots Dallman. Hear he's riding with you now."

Spur saw the man's whole body relax, but his hand stayed in place.

"Right, he's here. My name is Bennet. I run this spread. Sure as hell hope you're not going to sell Boots any more barbwire." The man grinned. "We kid him about sodbusting whenever we get the chance. Fact is he's a damn good farmer, and good with cattle too. Guess that's a smart combination the way the fence is going up around here."

"Progress, they say," Spur responded. "Any idea where I could find Boots?"

"Still gathering the strays this morning before we get the iron hot. I sent him and some men out south a little more. Should be cleaning out the second valley down that way with two more hands. Welcome to go take a look. Even welcome to help bring whatever you find back this way. Oh, I never got your name?"

"Brighten, Mack Brighten from out in Montana a ways."

"Well, good to meet you. Hope you find Boots. We really think a lot of that young man. He used to be one of my foremen."

Bennet touched his hat and rode back to the milling group of some fifty head of mixed cattle where they were held in a nervous group by six riders.

Spur found Boots riding sweep on a clutch of ten cows and half a dozen calves. The agent let the group ride past a patch of trees on the side of the valley, then Spur rode out and confronted Boots.

At first the man did not recognize McCoy.

"Boots Dallman?" Spur asked. He drew his Colt

.45 smoothly and had Dallman covered before he separated Spur from the morning sun behind him.

"Yeah, I'm Dallman. What's the iron for? Do I know you?"

"You saw me a few times." Spur rode to the side out of the direct path of the sun. "You might know me better with my hat off and with a rope around my neck!"

Dallman scowled and squinted.

"What is this, playing tricks time!"

"No trick, Dallman."

"My God! It's impossible! They hung you. You stopped twitching and we rode off! Either you're some kind of ghost or you didn't die."

"Ever see a ghost kill a man, Dallman?"

"Hey! No! I'm glad you're alive. Haven't had any sleep for a week worrying about that. I was drunk. The sheriff can tell you that. I didn't help them hang you!"

"Squirm, Dallman. I like to watch a man squirm who wouldn't even lift his voice to help me. You sat there on your horse and didn't say a word. Not one fucking word to help me!"

"I was scared! That Gabe Young is a madman. He would have shot me dead if I'd tried to save you."

"You don't have to be afraid of Young anymore. I hung him two days ago in Boise."

"You . . . you hung him?"

"Right, just the same way he hung me. Only he was robbing a bank at the time. It's going to be different with you. Probably hang you from that big beam in your barn. Your wife will have to watch of course."

"No! You've got no right!"

"Right? You're talking about rights after you lynched me and thought you watched me die? You knew I was goin' to die, still you didn't say a word. Dallman you have exactly no rights, no appeal, and no way to escape. You try to run and I grab your wife and kids. You try to bushwhack me and I'll come after you and slice your heart out. What would you do to the men who lynched you and left you for dead?''

Dallman's body sagged. His head lowered. When he looked up there were tears in his eyes. "I was drunk and weak and when I sobered up enough to know what was happening, you were already in the noose. Nothing I could have done then would have stopped them."

"You could have killed them both."

"I . . . I've never killed a man in my life. I was too young for the war. Since then . . .''

"You a Mormon or something?"

"No, I'm just not a violent man."

"Except when you're drunk and you lynch innocent people."

Boots looked away.

"Don't hurt Martha. I don't want you anywhere near my place. Do to me whatever you want, but don't hurt Martha or the boys. That's all I ask."

"I've got no argument with them. Dallman, let me tell you what it feels like to be hung, so you can think about it. I'm in no rush. You're not the kind of man who is going to hit the trail. And I don't think you'd draw on me if I turned my back. But you need to suffer. You can start thinking how it's going to feel to be hung, feel that rope burning your neck and cutting off your air, then the screaming agony as you hit the end of the rope and the knot that's supposed to break your neck doesn't and so you either die slowly of strangulation or brain damage when the blood is cut off."

Dallman motioned to the cattle now well ahead.
"I better get back to work."

"Worried about your job right up to the end, are
you Dallman? I'm going to hang you, Dallman, you
know that now, don't you. You probably should tell
your wife about it. She has a right to know why her
man is dead. Why he's hanging in the barn
twitching away the last spasms of his life."

"I might tell her."

"The rope burning your throat isn't the worst
part, Boots. The roughest time is when you feel your
eyes bulge out and you can't see anything. You
know your eyes are open, but they don't work anymore. Then your breath cuts off and your neck aches
with the strain of the knot. That's nothing of the
agony you're coming to, Dallman. Wait until the
blackness comes. That's the frightening part.

"The sky goes black and then you can TASTE the
blackness! You see shapes in the black void and you
know that death is sitting there right beside you,
ready to take over your body, AND THERE ISN'T
A DAMN THING YOU CAN DO ABOUT IT! That
is desperation, that is raw gut wrenching fear.
Because you know that this is all there is to life. The
religious fear of death syndrome you learned as a
child was only childish prattlings by adults. Now
you know the truth of death and you don't want to
give up those few seconds of life you have left. But
you will. Eternity, an eternity of dreamless sleep
beckons you, and then claims you . . .

"Then you will be dead, Boots Dallman. You will
cease to exist except as a memory, and perhaps a
photograph or two."

Spur looked at Boots. The crotch of his pants was
stained with a dark wetness.

"Happy dreams, Boots. The next time you see me,

I'll be an avenging angel arriving to hang you . . .
just the way you let them hang me!''

Dallman stared at him. Shifted on his saddle and
looked away. He slowly shook his head.

"You haven't even asked me why I wasn't dead
after the hanging. You deserve to know that. It was
the hangman's knot the sheriff tied. He did a
Murphy's knot and none of you knew the difference.
The Murphy does not break your neck, does not
strangle the person but puts enough pressure on the
carotid arteries going to the brain to make you
LOOK dead.''

Spur rode around the cowboy who had slumped
lower in the saddle.

"Dallman, you do whatever you want to, but don't
forget to tell your wife goodbye. You have no idea
how long it will be before I come back with a good
strong rope, and a well tied hangman's knot to
drop you into eternity!''

Spur stared at the cowboy, then turned and rode
away. As he expected, Boots Dallman did not try to
shoot him in the back.

12

As he rode back toward town from the Box B ranch, Spur McCoy began thinking about home, New York City. He hadn't been back there in years. The best part of his life had been working with the Secret Service.

Not that his home life had been hard or difficult. On the other hand it had been too easy. His father was a wealthy merchant and importer in the city, and they had three houses: a smart, efficient town house on Park Avenue, a country place out on Long Island, and a hide-a-way place of about fifteen rooms in Connecticut.

Spur's father expected him to take over the family businesses, and Spur was tempted. Wealth and all of the beautiful things it could buy, and the freedom it gave you pulled at him.

He went to Harvard and graduated half way up in his class, then came back to New York and worked in one of his father's importing houses for two years.

The Civil War was on the horizon and Spur took a

commission in the Infantry. After two years of
fighting he had advanced to the rank of captain.
Then he was called by a longtime family friend and
senior United States senator from New York,
Arthur B. Walton. The senator needed an aide,
somebody who knew what was going on in the war,
and who could talk back to the generals and their
wild demands. He enjoyed the work.

Then in 1865, soon after the act passed, Charles
Spur McCoy was appointed as one of the first U.S.
Secret Service Agents. Since the Secret Service was
the only federal law enforcement agency of any kind
at the time, it handled a wide range of problems,
most far removed from the group's original task of
preventing currency counterfeiting.

Spur served six months in the new Washington
Secret Service office, then was transferred to head
the base in St. Louis and handle all action west of
the Mississippi. He was chosen from ten men
because he was the one who could ride a horse best,
and he had won the service pistol marksmanship
contest. William P. Wood, the Agency director,
evidently thought both attributes would come in
handy out in the wilds of the West. He had been
right.

Spur's thoughts moved on to the case at hand and
Boots Dallman. The man certainly did not fit the
Gabe Young mold. He was contrite, he probably had
never been in trouble before and he said he was
drunk. Any man was allowed one character flaw—
unless it killed someone.

Being drunk for two days certainly was no excuse,
but it was at least a mitigating circumstance. Spur
would make up his mind about Dallman later.

Now he was headed for the lawyer in the case, the

husband of the delicious Eugenia Turner. Spur decided on the direct approach.

A half hour later Spur slapped the trail dust off his jeans and leather vest and walked up to the second floor office of Kane Turner. The sign on the door said: "Attorney at Law. Specializing in wills, civil and criminal law." That about covered the field.

He pushed open the door and went in. The room was twelve feet square, with a window looking down on a side street, a desk near the far wall and a chair for a guest. Two bookcases overflowed with law books, and a long table at one side was half filled with stacks of papers.

It was the first time Spur had met the man. He was two inches shy of six feet with dark black hair and wore a dark blue suit. Green eyes looked up at Spur. There was a moment of indecision, then a flash of recognition, and Turner stood slowly.

"Yes, good morning. I'm Kane Turner, attorney. Can I be of some help to you?"

"Sure hope so, Mr. Turner. I'm Spur McCoy, just in town a few days, and I'm thinking of settling down. I'll need a building I can use for a new gambling palace, a real classy, first rate place. It's gonna be better than anything in town now."

"A building. Well. I do know a little about the property here in town. Just how big a place do you want?" Turner waved him to a chair and they both sat down.

"Might consider one of the saloons if it's the right size. Need something on the ground floor, say fifty, sixty feet square, with back rooms and an upstairs I could use for cribs."

"That would be a large establishment," Turner

said. "I'll need to do some checking."

"Not giving you an order," Spur said. "Just looking around for somebody to do the legal work."

"Good. I'm the only real lawyer in town. I read for the law under Judge Anderson in Boise, so I am conversant with all the Idaho Territorial regulations and codes."

"Well, in that case, I might pick you to do my legal work."

They both laughed.

"I can assure you, Mr. McCoy, that I know the town as well as anyone here. I'll make some inquiries and have a report for you tomorrow about this time. If that would be soon enough."

"Suits me. I don't trust the looks of the three banks in town and I sure don't like keeping cash in a carpetbag. So the sooner the better." Spur glanced out the window.

"Looks of this town I'd think three or four thousand would buy what I want. What do you think?"

"Yes, prices are a little down right now with the way things been going. I'd say for four thousand we could get what you need. I have a place in mind . . . if the man will sell."

Spur rose, his dislike for the lawyer increasing. "Fine, tomorrow. I'll stop by after dinner."

They said goodbye and Spur went out to the steps and down to the dusty street. There was something about the man Spur did not like. The fact he was in on the counterfeiting had nothing to do with it.

The Secret Service agent shrugged, decided he was hungry and went back to the Pocatello Hotel dining room and had two portions of beef stew and applesauce for desert.

He went on to his room to change into a clean

shirt. This time the door was locked. He used his key and went in. Eugenia Turner lay on his bed, fully clothed. She heard him come in and sat up, sleep heavy in her eyes. She blinked and smiled.

"Sorry, guess I dozed off waiting for you. You don't spend much time in your room."

"I am a working man," he said.

She wore a white jacket and a silly little hat. Her dress was of some fine material that looked like a high fashion outfit. The black shoes were high button affairs.

"I brought you something," she said, smiling up at him. She opened her reticule and took out a sheaf of U.S. paper money and handed it to him.

They were twenties, banded with a piece of pink paper. He figured there were a hundred of them.

"That's two thousand dollars worth," she said smiling. "I like giving money away."

"Thanks, I always take a gift of two thousand in bogus money." He broke the band and leafed through the notes. Every one had the same serial number. The workmanship was excellent as the others had been. They probably all came from the same engraved plates. The work was done by an expert. He had the press, the pressman, and the lawyer. All he needed was the engraver. The man was an artist, and Spur bet this was not his first work at making counterfeit plates.

"Will that help you?"

"It takes a hundred of them out of possible circulation, so that is a help. I'd like the rest of them sometime, when your husband won't miss them."

"That would be hard. He looks at them every night."

"Oh." There was a pause that stretched out. He had no idea what else she might have on her mind, but he didn't want to suggest that the talk between them was over.

Eugenia smiled and put her reticule to one side. "It's a little warm in here," she said. Then she slipped out of the jacket, folded it carefully and put it on the bed. The dress under the jacket was for formal occasions. It was cut low with the edges of both her white breasts showing and the deepline of cleavage between them.

Spur grinned. "I like the dress," he said.

"I hoped that you would. A lady likes to be appreciated." She looked away and lifted her glance to the ceiling. "Oh, Lordy, I shouldn't have said that."

"Why not? It's true, and I am more than pleased to tell you you are a stunning woman, beautiful."

"Thank you. I usually don't go looking for compliments." She glanced at him. "I am a little confused."

"Why?"

"I don't know. I dressed up and fixed up just to come here and see you. The money was just an excuse. Now that I'm here, I feel all gay and girlish, like . . . like I was a virgin again and you were courting! Isn't that just the silliest thing!"

"I think it's sweet and flattering," Spur said. "May I sit down beside you?"

She caught her breath, and nodded.

He sat beside her so their thighs touched and she pulled away, then let the contact resume.

"Oh my!"

He touched her chin and lifted her face so she would look at him.

"Eugenia. Why did you come here?"

She sighed and looked away. He caught her chin and turned her face back to his.

"I . . . I'm not sure. I know I thought all night how it would feel if you . . . if you kissed me!"

"Easy," he said. Spur leaned in and kissed her. She met him halfway and just their lips touched. Her eyes were closed. Spur held the kiss as long as she did. Then they parted and her eyes came open slowly.

"Would you? . . . could we try that again?"

They kissed again and she made soft sounds deep in her throat. This time Spur put his arm round her and drew her close to him, her breasts touching his chest. The kiss was longer and when it ended she snuggled against him. She spoke softly without looking at him.

"I think, Spur McCoy, that I came here to get even with my husband. I know he's had other women. I just wondered . . . I mean . . . Oh, damn!"

He held her, then tenderly put his hand over one of her half exposed breasts.

"Oh, Lordy!" she whispered. Eugenia shivered, then reached to kiss him again. This time when his lips met hers, they were parted and Spur's tongue slid into her mouth and she moaned and he felt her hips move against him.

His hand massaged the soft, whiteness of her breast, then edged under the fabric until he had her whole breast in his hand.

Slowly he eased backward on the bed and brought her with him. She pushed over more until she lay fully on top of him. Her eyes came open and she stared down at him. His hand was still inside her dress top, massaging the warming breast.

"Oh, Lordy!" she said.

Spur lifted up and kissed the side of her breast and he felt her shiver again. Her whole body vibrated for a moment and then she opened her eyes.

"Nobody has ever . . . I mean Kane isn't very romantic. He just thinks about his own . . . needs."

"The man is an idiot," Spur growled. He moved his hand from her breast and found the fasteners on the dress in back and opened it to her waist, then slid the fabric off her shoulders. The dress had a sewn in chemise of some sort and when he pushed the cloth down, it left her bare to the waist.

"I really shouldn't," she whispered, biting her lip. Her wide set brown eyes blinked back the start of tears. He smoothed her long black hair that showered around her bare shoulders now like black rain.

Spur used both hands and fondled her hanging breasts. Until now he had not realized how full they were, like a pair of small melons waiting to be picked. Her eyes glowed as he warmed her breasts. The light pink areolas took on a deeper shade and her small nipples stiffened and stood taller with hot blood surging into them.

Spur reached up and kissed one breast, then licked her nipple and bit it gently.

"Oh, God, but that is marvelous!" she whispered. Then her body jolted in a series of spasms as she climaxed. She fell on him, her breasts crushed against him as she climaxed three times bringing tears of joy to her eyes, and a gasping, desperation to try to pump enough oxygen into her bloodstream to supply her vibrating muscles.

When the spasms passed she lifted up from him and stared down.

"I've never done . . . That's the very first time I've ever done that so soon. You weren't even undressed. I mean . . ." the blush colored her neck and chest red.

Spur chuckled and kissed her other breast, then rolled her beside him on the bed. She began unbuttoning his vest and his shirt at once, and smiled in delight as she found black hair on his chest she could twirl and play with.

"Could we get out of the rest of our clothes?" she asked.

"That sounds interesting," Spur said. She sat up and pulled the dress over her head, then sat there watching him.

She still wore the conventional drawers, knee length underwear that clung tightly to the body, with a draw string at the top and a six inch ruffle of embroidery around the bottom of each leg. A dozen pink bows decorated the white lawn material.

He enjoyed the way the movement made her breasts roll and bounce. He slipped out of his shirt, then kicked off his boots and socks and pulled down his denim pants. This time Spur wore no underwear and she gasped as she saw his genitals spring fully ready from the fabric.

"Oh, Lordy!" She said. "I had no idea . . . ! I mean Kane's is so small compared . . ." She laughed.

He put his hands on her drawers and untied the draw string. Her hand covered hers.

"I'm not ready. Play with me more."

He lay on his back and pulled her down over him, then let her dip one breast into his mouth. He licked it and then sucked all he could into his mouth and chewed tenderly. He switched and then put his hands on her rounded buttocks.

"I could spank you," he said.

She frowned. "Why?"

"You've never been spanked . . . this way?"

She shook her head.

"You'll like it." He began softly at first then harder until she tenderly growled and nipped at him with her teeth.

"That is wonderful! Why didn't somebody tell me before!"

She rolled over and smiled at him. He lowered toward her, his lips kissing her breasts, then moving down to her waist. She gasped as he lifted the edge of her drawers and kissed under it.

Slowly Spur pulled down the loosened drawers, kissing them lower and lower.

When he came to the edge of her pubic hair she held his face.

"That's far enough, for right now. I'll take them off. Damn! I'll rip them off if I have to!"

A moment later she was naked, writhing slowly as she lay beside him.

She leaned over and kissed his lips and watched him when she came away. "I've never wanted to make love before so much in my life! You have just set me on fire!"

"Good. It should always be that way." He nibbled at her lips, then let his hand fondle her breasts and move lower.

"Oh, Lordy!" she said softly as his fingers crept through her protecting "V" of soft fur at her crotch.

Her own hand slid over toward him and rubbed his chest, then moved lower and she gasped as she found his erect penis.

"I don't believe it! I don't see how any man could have one this huge! Beautiful! He is just absolutely amazingly beautiful!"

His hand parted the fur and stroked around her moist center. Eugenia gasped.

"Oh, yes! Darling, yes! Right now. Not another second to waste. We've wasted too much time already. Now! Right now!"

She tugged at him to come over her. He went between her spread legs, her knees were lifted and he bent, then touched her and thrust, came back, and thrust again and she yelped in delight.

"Yes! Inside! Yes! More, more!"

Then it was one short race to the finish line. Eugenia was so worked up that she climaxed the moment he was fully in her and three more times.

Spur worked at his own pace, but soon found he was speeding up to match her movements. He charged, then sprinted and at last he was pounding with a vengeance until he erupted and her feet were locked over his back riding him from below until she squeezed every drop of fluid from him.

He fell on her heavily and she grunted, then smiled, and they both closed their eyes and rested.

Ten minutes later she roused and kissed his cheek.

"Again" she said.

Spur grinned, lifted and began stroking until he felt the juices surging. It was a repeat performance. They both were sweating by then, wetness dripping from Spur's nose and chin onto her face, their bodies glued together with salt tinged perspiration.

They both exploded at the same time. Eugenia screeched in wonder and awe and delight and Spur rumbled until he had driven the last of his seed into her fertile soil.

They slept a half hour this time and when she roused, Spur had sat up and smoked half way down on a thin black cigar.

She snuggled against him, licking his side, looking up.

"Can I snuggle into your pocket and stay with you always?" she asked.

"What would your husband say?"

"He's going to be in prison anyway."

"Probably."

"So can I go with you?"

"No."

She scowled, stuck her tongue out at him. "Just a *No*? No explanation? I'm throwing my body at your feet and you step on me?"

He kissed her forehead. "Not at all, I'm thinking what will be best for you."

"Sure you are. You have just spoiled me for any ordinary man. I'll always compare their lovemaking to yours and it will be lacking."

"Not true. You're just starting to awaken. You'll make any man a better lover now. You know you will be."

"I want to keep you."

"I'm a fiddlefoot. A rover. I'm never in one place more than a week at a time."

"I like to travel."

"I sleep outdoors more than in a bed."

"Oh."

"People keep trying to kill me."

"Oh."

"I never make much money."

"Oh."

"I spend half my travel time on horseback."

"I don't like to ride."

"So?"

"So, maybe I can't go with you," she said, tears wetting her cheeks.

"Maybe so. But you could come back to my room again before I go."

"And stay all night?"

"We'll see."

She cried as she dressed, then clung to him as they walked to the door. She reached up and kissed him again.

"Spur McCoy, no matter what else I do, I'll always love you, always want you." She bit her lip so she couldn't say anything more, turned and went out the doorway into the hall, holding her small shoulders straight and stiff so she would not turn to look back at him.

Spur watched her walk down the hall, then turn toward the front door. She never did look back.

13

Spur dressed slowly, thinking about the sexy and complicated woman called Eugenia Turner. He decided she would not be a problem no matter what happened to her husband. She had decided she must act concerning the counterfeiting and she had. Now she would let the drama run its course and take the consequences even if they meant hardship for her.

McCoy turned his thinking to his next move. He had only two men involved so far in the conspiracy. Something this big must have more people taking part than that. He needed the rest of the participants. There had to be at least one more man in on the plot. Spur did as he so often did, strike at the weak link in the other camp.

It was a little after three that afternoon when Spur walked up to the newspaper office. J. Larson Wintergarden was not there. A note on the door said he was out on business and would return before five that afternoon.

Spur looked through the window, scowled and

thought of going to the Mercantile and harrasssing Joshua Hoffer, but he was saving that for an all day affair. Instead he went to Doc Rawson's office and let the sawbones take a look at his injured flesh.

The old doctor mumbled as he checked Spur's leg.

"Glad to see you've been staying off it, like I told you," he said sarcastically. Doc Rawson shook his head. "Damn fool! Part of it's busted lose again. When you gonna learn?"

"When they plow me under about six feet, I reckon, Doc. Did you know much at my age?"

Rawson chuckled. "Hell no, still can't brag about my smarts. But dang-blasted, McCoy. You could loose that leg."

"You're just trying to scare me, old man. What does my neck look like? You ever make love with a bandage around your neck?"

"So that's what's bothering you." He took off the wrappings and nodded.

"Yep. Yep."

"So what does that mean?"

"Mean, yep, or yes, or some such nonsense."

He used an instrument and picked off dead skin from Spur's neck. "Healing up better than I expected. Figured you'd have a nice furrow across your throat to the day you stop breathing, but don't look like it now."

"Let me look," Spur said.

The doctor found a hand glass and Spur stared at his neck and the ugly red flesh. Some of it had healed, the edges, but the raw open wound was still there.

"Six weeks, son," Doc Rawson said. "Six, maybe seven before you can go without some kind of a bandage on there. Your sex life might have to

suffer for a while if'n you can't function with your
neck wrapped."

"Didn't say couldn't."

"Yeah, rightly, rightly. Didn't say wouldn't
either."

They both laughed.

Doc Rawson went to work then, putting some
ointment on Spur's neck and wrapping it up
securely. Then he pressed the wound in his leg
together again and bandaged it.

When he was done he sat back and motioned for
Spur to put on his pants.

"Couple of years you should be good as new, depending on how good that was way back then."

"Better than I remember, Doc."

Spur handed him a five dollar gold piece and
waved off any change. "I'll charge it to Uncle Sam
anyway, the government has lots of money."

"I don't send them any," Doc said. He frowned
slightly and waved. "Get out of here and don't get
yourself shot up again."

Spur wandered around the small town, had a cold
beer at a saloon and watched some gamblers work
the dollar bet table. Then he headed toward the
newspaper office.

He arrived about 4:30 and saw the note gone from
the door. When he pushed inside he found Wintergarden coming in from the back shop. His hands
were black with ink and he wore a green visor.

"Yes sir? Oh, Mr. McCoy, the man who buys
newspapers. Am I still in business?" He smiled at
the little joke.

Spur did not smile.

"You may be out of business in a few minutes.
You printed these on your Isaac Adams, and I want

to know everyone who worked with you."

Spur spread out three of the twenty dollar bills on the counter top.

"You'll notice that each bill has the same serial number, the giveaway in counterfeiting."

Wintergarden made a strange little noise in his throat and started to step back, but Spur grabbed him by the shirt front and pulled him against the near side of the counter.

"I don't know what you're saying. I deal in facts and news stories. I'm just a newspaper man."

"Yeah, one with a past. I'd put a year's pay on a bet that you have a record, that you've printed funny money like this before somewhere back East."

"No!"

"Too quick with the denial, little man. You have the only press this side of Chicago that could do this print job. It's extremely well done, a masterful job. First you dig out the engraved plates you printed from and then you tell me who you're working with."

"I tell you I'm just a news man with a small paper that is almost ready to make money. If I can hold on another three or four years this town is going to grow. Railroad might even come through . . . "

Spur let go of him, went around the counter and into the back shop.

"Plates must be back here somewhere."

The back shop was like most of the others he had seen. The job press with a place of honor, stacks of paper and racks with more sheets in it. A hand cranked paper cutter thirty-six inches wide, the big flat bed press where the newspaper was printed, a barrel of ink, and dozens and dozens of small boxes.

Against the wall stood a type cabinet. It was five

feet high and had slots where fonts of type were slid in each in its own type case made of wood. Each case was divided into dozens of small spaces where the individual letters for that size and style of type were "cased."

Depending on the size and style of type, there could be two or three thousand individual metal letters in each drawer.

"Maybe you hid the plates in one of these type drawers." Spur pulled out one of the wooden drawers two feet by three feet and dumped it on the floor.

"Oh, oh, I pied the type," Spur said.

"Stop it! I don't have the plates. They took them with them."

"Then you did print the money, you did the counterfeiting?"

"Only the printing. They watched me carefully. And I only get a hundred dollars a month of the money to spend."

"Why?"

"Does it matter?"

"It does to me. Why?"

"I got in trouble back in Illinois, like you said. Printing again, green ink from some artistic plates that were not good enough."

"How long?"

"Five years, with two months off for good behavior. I ran the prison printing plant. I'm an excellent printer."

"You proved that. Let's go back up front. I want you to write out what you've told me, all of it."

"The others will be furious."

"Won't matter, Wintergarden, they'll be in jail too. Start writing."

Spur read it as he wrote. He used no names except

his own. When it was all down, Spur had him sign it. Then read through it again, and Spur signed and dated it.

"Good, it's all there except the names. Who are the rest of them? I know about Kane Turner. Who else is in on the scheme?"

"I'll tell you as soon as I'm in jail. I don't trust them."

"Fair enough. Nobody says you have to get killed. How many more are there?"

"Just one."

"Fine that makes it easier. Anything you want to take with you to jail? You could be gone for some time, I'd guess fifteen to twenty this time."

Wintergarden shook his head, looked around one last time and opened the front door.

The shot came from outside, blasted twice and pounded Wintergarden backward, falling against Spur and they both went down on the wooden floor in a tangle. By the time Spur jumped up and got to the door, he could see no one with a gun out and no one running away.

There were few people on the street. A man hurried up panting from the run.

"I saw the bastard! He ran around the back of the shop. Wasn't such a big guy, but I was too far away to see who he was."

Spur sprinted in the direction the man pointed. No one was in the alley, there were a dozen other shops and stores on this side of the alley, and six houses on the far side. The killer could have escaped into any one of them.

Back at the print shop, a crowd had gathered. The sheriff elbowed his way through and checked Wintergarden.

"Dead," he said.

A flurry of talk went through the crowd. Spur took the sheriff in the back part of the print shop and told him what happened.

Sheriff Sloan nodded. "This the real reason you came to town?"

"Right, and it's not ready to end here. I need another day or two. When I find the man who killed Wintergarden there, I'll have the other man I want."

"You're not telling me the whole story, are you, McCoy?"

"Not until I get the other man. For all I know it could be you." He grinned. "Sheriff, you'll get the arrest and the credit for wrapping this up, just as soon as it's done."

Sheriff Sloan's hand hovered over his pistol. "I could take you in and lock you up until you talk."

"Could, but won't."

"Why?"

"Because I'm a lawman, too, and you've never drawn on another lawman, have you, Sheriff?" Spur's stare was cold, hard.

"Can't say as I have. Guess I won't this time, either." He grinned and relaxed his hand over the gun. "But make it quick as you can. Folks around here like their killings solved fast."

Spur left the room and worked through the crowd. The town's barber and undertaker was officiating as two men carried the body down the block to the undertaking parlor.

By the time Spur got to the law office of Kane Turner, the door was closed and locked. It was a little after 5:30. He asked two people on the street before one knew where the Turners lived. It was only three blocks away.

When Spur came to the house he saw three

buggies drawn up to the side of the street in front of the residence.

Lights glowed all over the three story wooden structure and he could hear the music of a piano. Spur marched up the sidewalk and rang a twist bell.

Kane Turner came to the door, saw Spur and lifted his eyebrows in surprise.

"Mr. McCoy? This is a surprise. Are you in a hurry to find out what I did today about your building."

"Not really. I'm more interested in retaining you in a personal matter. I was almost a witness to a shooting tonight. The sheriff was not friendly. If I am charged with anything, will you represent me in court?"

"Of course! A killing. I hadn't heard. We've had this dinner planned for weeks and I came home early to help Eugenia and the cook and to greet the guests. They came about 4:30." He paused. "Do you know who was killed?"

"A man by the name of Wintergarden, I understand, the newspaper man."

Spur saw Turner's eyes close into a squint, his mouth came open in surprise, then he recovered.

"Yes, I know him, good printer, fair news man. But he's dead now, you say?"

"I'm afraid so. Well, I'll let you get back to your guests. Just wanted to be sure you were my lawyer in case I need one."

"Of course, and thanks."

They nodded and Spur walked down the steps to the sidewalk and out to the dirt street. He kept going for half a block to the end, then doublebacked and hurried down an alley so he could see both the front and rear entrances to the big Turner house.

The lawyer could not have shot Wintergarden. He

was truly shocked at the news. He had five or six witnesses for the time of the killing. But Turner would have an idea who might have killed the printer. THEIR printer!

Spur did not think it would be a long wait. Turner would be as anxious as Spur was to learn for sure who had pulled the trigger twice.

The Secret Service Agent leaned against a tree in the alley and waited. It was fully dark now. Spur edged around the tree so he could see better.

Just then the rear door of the Turner place opened quietly, a figure slipped out and walked quickly down the alley toward where Spur hid.

14

The Secret Service Agent edged around the big tree he had been hiding behind as the figure of a man walked toward him down the alley, then past.

The man was Kane Turner, no mistake.

When the black shadow on black alley moved close to the street, Spur followed him. It was a simple task, not once did Turner look back to see if anyone were behind him.

He walked quickly to the end of the next block, then out a lane that had little suggestion that any official street work had ever been done on it. Only two houses were on the track. They sat back from the other residences, as if to say by positioning that they were superior.

From a quick look at the size and spread of the places, they were probably the biggest and best homes in Twin Falls. Turner went to the front door, knocked and waited. A few moments later the door opened and he vanished inside.

Spur found a good place to sit down and waited.

The Big Dipper made a two hour move around the North star and Spur decided he had watched long enough. Whatever was going on had not turned violent but didn't seem to be ending quickly, either.

McCoy went back to his hotel, found his room unoccupied, washed up in the heavy china bowl with the tepid water, and fell on the bed naked to try to sleep. The weather had turned warm and the nights had not cooled down that much.

In the morning, McCoy was up at dawn as usual, shaved, washed off his upper body and put on a clean shirt. He would have to hunt up a laundry if he were in town much longer. He checked his carpetbag and decided now was the time. Spur chuckled at the heroic image he made stuffing dirty laundry into the pillow case from the bed. Not at all what he had in mind when he signed up for this glorious life as a Secret Service Agent.

The clerk told him where he could get his laundry done. It was a combination dry goods store and laundry just down the block. At the counter where he left his laundry a wide eyed girl with a big grin winked at him.

"Hi, new in town I bet, and not married or you wouldn't bring us your dirty socks, right?" She had deep green eyes, a turned up nose and her peasant white blouse clung to large, firm breasts.

"Caught me. Just don't starch my socks."

She laughed and bent over to look in the sack. It let her blouse fall forward and Spur found himself staring straight down the open blouse at her breasts that swung and swayed under the blouse with nothing else covering them.

She glanced up at him without moving.

"See anything you like," she asked softly.

"I see two beauties I like," he said so no one else could hear.

She leaned back so the blouse covered her again. "The laundry will cost you sixty-five cents. Those other things you like are three dollars—but you get dinner and drinks at my place. How about tonight?"

"Sorry, I have to see a lady about her pet bird."

The girl laughed. "You talk crazy. I've got a wild bird, you want to see her dance?"

"Next time, pretty lady. When will my socks be starched and ready to pick up?"

"This afternoon, about 4:30 if you're in a rush. Or at my place at 6:30 if you're in no hurry."

"Right, 4:30. I'll be here."

"Damn, I could come down to two dollars."

"Never cut your prices, little darling, it's bad for business." Spur patted her shoulder and went out into the sunshine.

It was going to be hot again today.

A dust devil three feet wide spun its corkscrew journey across the street.

A woman's sunbonnet went sailing down the boardwalk.

Spur moved out toward the big house on the lane just north of most of the town. When he was within sight of it, he saw a woman watering scraggly flowers in her front yard.

"Beg your pardon, Ma'am," Spur said.

She turned, frowning. She was about thirty, plain, wearing a simple print dress that covered her chin to wrist and dragged in the dust.

"I ain't buying nothing more. After I got those hair brushes my Charley fairly threw me out of the house. He said . . ." She stopped. "Oh, you're not the same drummer."

"No Ma'am. Just wanted to know who lives in

that first house down there, the big one on the lane?''

"Everybody knows that, so you must be a stranger. You mean them folks any harm?''

"No, Ma'am. I was just wondering if the house was for sale?''

"Don't rightly know. Might ask at the Mercantile, the Hoffer Mercantile. He owns it. Lives in the house. But he don't treat his wife right. I see the poor thing crying behind that big window just lots of times.''

"Yes, Ma'am. I feel like crying sometimes myself.'' He watched her look up, surprised. He touched the brim of his low crowned brown hat with the silver pesos around it, and walked back toward town.

Hoffer! The man could be hanged only once. If he tied in with the counterfeiters, he must be the most important one, or the only other one. He could be the engraver. Or the plates could have been produced elsewhere and brought here. No, engravers were artists, but they were also vain and selfish.

If Hoffer made the plates, he would not let them out of his sight, not even when they were being used to print the bogus money. The engraver must come from right here in town. Chances are it was Hoffer.

On his way back to Hoffer's store, Spur saw that the newspaper office was closed and padlocked. There was a notice on the door that anyone who had any claim against H. Larson Wintergarden or his newspaper, should file his claim with the sheriff's office within ten days.

Spur read the notice again. That could mean there were no known relatives, and that the county had taken charge of the property.

He continued to the Mercantile and walked in the

front door. This time he made no effort to avoid the small, fat man who worked behind the counter. Hoffer looked up as Spur stood across the counter from him.

The merchant's small green eyes under the thinning brown hair, stared at the Agent.

"Yes sir. How may I help you?"

The nervous tick over Hoffer's right eye pulsated once, then remained inactive.

Spur nodded. "Yes, it had to be you."

"What? I don't understand."

"Of course you do, Hoffer. I was standing beside Wintergarden when you shot him. I saw you through the window, then I saw you outside running down the alley. Not hard to miss that limp-legged way you run."

"You're saying that I shot . . . Ridiculous, simply ridiculous. I'm a busy man and don't have time for wild stories. If you'll kindly remove yourself from the premises . . ."

Spur put one big hand around the merchant's throat from the front and squeezed both sides.

"I could kill you this way in about three minutes, Hoffer. Cuts off all the blood supply to the brain. Almost like being hung. Now think again about the shooting. I saw you, how can you deny it?"

Hoffer's face grew redder as the seconds ticked by. Before he passed out, Spur let up on the pressure, and moved his big hand.

"Oh, God . . . oh, God!" Hoffer's voice came out soft, garbled. A minute later he could speak normally.

"You get out of here! I've got a shotgun in back of the counter, and I'll shoot you down in a minute and never be sorry!"

"You probably never are sorry, Hoffer. You shot

Wintergarden, didn't you?"

"Of course not. I don't care what he prints in his silly little newspaper. Nobody reads it anyway."

"I read it, Hoffer, and it tells me a lot about you."

Hoffer stared at him, still massaging his sore throat.

"Hoffer, I'd say you spent three to five years in Midvale Federal prison for forgery. That come close?"

"Absolutely not! I am not a convict, I've never been in prison."

"I can get the records. Changed your name, of course, but I can find it. Doesn't matter that much. It wasn't what Wintergarden printed in his paper that you objected to, it was what he talked to me about the day before he was killed."

"Lies, all lies! I don't have to put up with this."

"Are you going to run away, again, Hoffer? You did last time. A new state, a new name, and some of the old money to get a new start. Then the old itch comes back. Hard to get rid of completely, isn't it?"

"What the hell are you talking about?"

"Bringing in that Isaac Adams press was the first mistake. It's the first thing we watch for."

Hoffer began looking around, his eyes darting to the counter top.

"Don't reach for that shotgun or you'll be a dead man before you hit the floor!"

Hoffer stared at him blankly.

Spur took two twenty dollar bills from his pocket and laid them on the counter top.

"Notice the serial numbers on both bills, Mr. Hoffer. You'll see they are exactly the same. We can't expect you to stop the press and engrave a new number for every bill, can we?"

Hoffer slumped on the counter.

Spur shook his head. "Only a matter of time, Hoffer. I find those plates here in your store, you are a dead man. You thought Wintergarden was going to talk, that's why you shot him. Now you're worried about Kane Turner blasting you when you walk out the door tonight. Could happen. You two on best of terms, I hope."

Hoffer glared at Spur. "If you have any evidence, you just go ahead and arrest me. Otherwise you get out of my store!" Hoffer got back some of his courage. "You had proof you wouldn't be jawboning me this way. Yeah, you're fishing!"

Spur reached up and took the neckerchief down from where it had been covering his bandaged neck. He removed his hat and stared at Hoffer.

"Ever seen me before, Hoffer?"

"Course not, you're a stranger in . . ."

He squinted his green eyes and looked at Spur's neck.

"What happened to your neck?"

"Bad burn, a rope burn. I was the guest of honor at a lynching one morning out east of town. Remember it, Hoffer?"

"My God! NO! It can't be. You was dead! Damn eyes bulged out, and you was hanging there." He took two steps back until he hit the wall. "Now, look here. That lynching was Gabe Young's idea. You was there. He had the gun. He had ALL OF US under his gun. Me and that ranch kid, Boots, we couldn't do nothing!"

You *helped him* you bastard. You jabbed your knife into my horse and made her race out from under me. *You were my hangman!*"

Hoffer was shaking now. Spittle drooled down the

side of his chin. His eyes were wild. He kept looking at the place under the counter where the shotgun must be.

"Hoffer, think back. Young didn't have you under his gun. You were enjoying yourself, laughing, teasing Boots. Hell, you said you enjoy a good hanging."

"No . . . no!"

"Yes, yes, Hoffer! You hung me, you bastard!"

"Get Gabe Young! He done it. Gabe's fault."

"You can tell him that, Hoffer, next time you two talk in hell. I hung Gabe in Boise a few days ago. He was robbing a bank at the time. Might say I killed two snakes with the same rope."

Hoffer mumbled something and leaned against the wall, then slid down it slowly until he slumped to a sitting position on the floor.

"All Gabe's idea! All Gabe's . . ."

"Ever wonder what it feels like to be hung, Hoffer? You should know because one of these days you're going to find out in person. Just having that noose lower over your head is the worst part, because it's the start of the end of your life. The rope is over the limb and tied off tight, the rope's been tested, no way it's going to slip or break. And there you are staring at the last few seconds of your *entire life!*"

"No! No more. Don't tell me."

"Afraid, Hoffer? Good. Sweat you bastard! Every day and every night you're going to be thinking about being hung, and knowing that I'm out there waiting for exactly the right time. Yeah, Hoffer, you're right. I'm a lawman, a federal lawman, and I believe in the law and justice. But this time it's Spur McCoy's law, and Spur McCoy's justice, because it was Spur McCoy's neck that got stretched by your rope!" Spur watched him on the floor. He had laid down now and curled into a ball as tight as he could. The fetal position, he was trying to go back to his mother's womb for protection.

"Leaves you with an interesting decision to make, Hoffer. You can go to the sheriff and admit that you murdered H.L. Wintergarden. That way you'll have the sheriff's protection when he jails you. After that all you have to do is try to beat the murder charge. If you do, I'll still be around to stretch your neck with a stout rope. Of course, if they convict you of murder, the sheriff will get the honor of dropping the trap on you up there on the scaffold."

Spur pushed his toe into the balled up little merchant.

"Make up your mind you lynching little sonofabitch! You don't have much longer." Spur turned and walked out of the store.

15

By noon that day, Spur McCoy was in a smattering of brush a quarter of a mile behind the Boots Dallman ranch. He had checked at the Box B spread and the ramrod said Boots had gone home the day before. He looked as slick as a year old orphaned heifer.

Spur pulled out a pair of battered but still workable ex-army binoculars and studied the small farmranch layout. A woman came out of the back door of the house, shook a dust mop, stared at the vegetable garden down by the creek, and retreated into the shade of the structure.

Ten minutes later a man came out. He had a small limp as he moved to the barn. He was as tall as a new-split rail and blond—Boots Dallman for sure.

Spur waited until he was in the barn, then went along the small line of brush next to the creek that swept within twenty yards of the back of the barn. With the building between him and the house, Spur walked to the unpainted excuse for a barn and slid in a back door. He carried a coil of new, half inch rope. On one end hung a hangman's noose with thirteen wraps.

Dallman was pitching hay into a stall with two milk cows waiting.

Spur's Colt .45 came in his hand and as he walked up he pulled the hammer back.

The clicking of the metal on metal made a deadly sound in the quietness of the barn. Dallman froze when he heard the sound and turned slowly, his hands still on the four-tined pitchfork.

"Put the fork down easy like," Spur said.

Dallman looked at him with hollow eyes, nodded, then dropped the haying tool that could also be a deadly weapon.

"Figured you'd come when I wasn't alooking. McCoy, wasn't it?" Dallman's eyes were bloodshot, sagging black half circles showed beneath his lids. His hands plucked at each other as if they were finding lice.

"A man should remember the name of everyone he lynches, Dallman. How has it been these past couple of days knowing that at any time you might turn around and see me holding a noose made from a sturdy half inch hemp rope?"

"It's been pure hell, McCoy. I ain't slept for three nights running now. Better I just keep working so things will be easier for Martha when I'm . . . after I . . ."

"After you're hung and dead and buried. No sense putting it off any longer. Get one horse and bring it around back. I'll have you in my sights all the time. Just put the bridle on it. Dallman, I'm good with this .45."

Boots watched him with furious eyes, yet there was no violence in the man. Slowly he nodded.

"Time for me to say goodbye to my family?"

"Did you give me time for that, Dallman?"

"Reckon we didn't."

"You remember that much. Get moving, Dallman. We'll go out from the back of the barn so Martha won't get curious, won't unlimber a Sharps at us. I've seen some Western women who were damn fine shots."

"Martha don't like guns." Dallman stared at Spur, then went down the alley of the barn to the far stalls, put a bridle on a horse and led it to the back door.

He looked at Spur. "You ready?"

"Damn right. I got hung once, now it's your turn."

They walked out the back door of the barn. Spur did not bother to close it. They went across the field two hundred yards to a scraggly maple tree that had a solid limb about the right height.

Spur threw the noose over the overhanging limb on the first try, raised it ten feet off the ground and belayed the end of the rope around the base of the maple tree and tied it off tightly.

"Sit down over there and wait," he told Boots.

Spur jumped on the back of the saddleless horse, caught the noose and held the rope above the big slip knot. He put his weight on it and hung there by his hands a moment to be sure it would not slip.

Boots looked up.

"Not even a Murphy's knot?"

"You know damn well it isn't, Boots. You only get one chance when you kill a man, or when you try damn hard and miss like you did. Then you pay the price."

"Don't you think I've thought of that for the past few days! I've been in a living hell! Almost glad that it will be over. Martha ain't been too happy with me neither. I was stone dead drunk walking those two days with the posse but I didn't know what the hell I was doing. Told you that. Told you I get drunk about twice a year. Martha understands!''

"I didn't understand, Boots! Not when that rope seared my neck and cut off my air and damn near broke my neck! I didn't understand it when I passed out and didn't know a fucking thing until Sheriff Sloan cut me down and slapped me awake. Even then I thought I was dead! I sure as hell didn't understand!''

Spur dropped off the rope and went to the tree.

"Just to make damn sure this thing holds. Hate like hell to bungle it as bad as you guys did and have to shoot you." Spur looked at the rope where it was tied behind the tree. He paused a minute, then came back.

"Might as well get it over with. Get up on the horse, Boots, then put the noose around your neck and cinch it up.''

"I got to hang myself?''

"Almost. I'll help on the tough parts.''

Boots jumped on the horse, moved her under the noose and pulled it down so his head would go through the opening. He glared at Spur, then shrugged.

"Tell . . . Tell Martha I'm damn sorry it ended this way. I tried. Tried like hell. Just one stupid mistake . . .'' He wiped away wetness from his eyes. "Tell her I love her and the kids.''

Spur nodded.

"Guess it's time, Boots. You're going to find out what it feels like to be hung. What is it the sheriff always says, 'May God have mercy on your soul.' ''

Spur tied Boots' hands behind his back, then looked up at the haggard man.

"Remember, Boots, you earned this," Spur said. He whacked his flat hand against the rump of the mare and she bolted forward.

Without the saddle to hold him, Boots skidded off the hind quarters of the mare at once, the rope tightened and he fell a foot before it took up the slack. Boots screamed and all the anguish and anger and shame and fury of what he done poured out.

Then the rope gave way behind the tree and it snaked across the limb. Boots Dallman fell three feet to the ground. His boots hit and he buckled forward, skidding in the dust.

Spur squatted down beside the cowboy-farmer who lay in the dust under the maple tree. His face was wet with tears. Spur cut the rawhide that held his hands together and Boots sat up. His eyes were still closed.

"Dear God, I hit the ground, I can't be dead!"

"Not unless dropping three feet is going to kill your boots," Spur said. "You're as alive as you ever were. Maybe a little smarter now."

Boots wiped the tears away and opened his eyes, staring at Spur with only a slight frown.

"Why?"

"I believed you. I believed what the sheriff said about you. Remembering back, I couldn't remember what you did during my own hanging. You did nothing. You didn't even hold their coats, but at least you didn't help the bastards."

"But I didn't try to stop them."

"The law doesn't say you have to be a hero, or be a brave man."

"Gabe Young?"

"I hanged him, in the bank in Boise. He and four others were robbing it late one night."

"Josh Hoffer?"

"I still have plans for him."

"I'd rather not know."

"How did you like being almost hung, Boots?"

"Terror. Stark, total, unrelenting, massive, hellish terror." He looked at Spur. "You know that better than I do. I don't blame you, McCoy. I'd want to do the same thing if I had been in your place. Know one thing for damned certain. I'm never going to touch another drop of booze for as long as I live!"

"With your capacity, that sounds like a good idea," Spur said.

They both saw her at the same time. Martha Dallman walked across the field toward them. They waited, Spur squatting, Boots sitting in the dust, the noose still around his neck.

"You cut the rope when you went over to check?"

"True. All but one tiny strand that I knew wouldn't hold your weight. I did want to scare the shit out of you."

"Damned well did that."

Martha came up to them and looked at both.

"I still have a husband, good."

Boots pulled the noose open and took it off his head. He threw it at the tree.

"Mr. McCoy, Boots told me all about it. I know the whole story. I saw most of what happened here from the barn. Got curious why Boots was gone so long. Want to tell you that I had the rifle, but I didn't shoot." She laughed softly. "But that was only because I was afraid I might hit my husband."

"Yes, Ma'am," Spur said. He was uneasy. The lesson was learned. He wanted to move back to town.

"Come down to the house, both of you. There's something I have to do."

"Mrs. Dallman, I better get on back to town."

"This is something that needs to be done. It must be accomplished now, Mr. McCoy. Long overdue. I hope you don't mind."

"Yes, Ma'am."

They walked toward the barn. The horse was a quarter of a mile down the valley where she had run, but she would be back for oats when it got dark. Spur walked slightly behind the other two, but they did not talk. No one said a word until they stepped into the farmhouse kitchen.

It was neat, clean and a pot of coffee simmered on a wood burning cookstove.

Martha Dallman poured a cup of coffee and took it to her husband.

"Boots, I want you to sit right there at the table and not say a word. No matter what happens you say a single word and I'll divorce you and take the kids and go back to Illinois. You understand Bobby Lee Dallman?"

His eyes widened as she used his given names. He nodded.

She turned and poured a second cup of coffee and handed this one to Spur who stood at one side.

He sipped at it and was about to say something when she spoke again.

"Mr. McCoy, Boots does get a wild streak now and again and thinks he needs a night in town. He goes in, gets liquored up and then jumps one of them fancy women in a saloon. Last time I warned him. I told him one more time and I was going to get me a lover and do it and tell him about it.

"That was before I knew about him going on that posse that turned into the lynching party. Now I figure it's time to pay back Boots Dallman."

Martha wore a green blouse that buttoned to the throat and a long green skirt that covered her ankles. Now she smiled at Spur and began unbuttoning her blouse.

"I hear some men think it's torture to watch while someone else makes love to their wife. I'm sure Boots thinks so. Mr. McCoy could you do me the honor of fucking me right now while Boots watches? It would be like a double payment to him and I would be highly thankful."

"No, I'm afraid not. I evened the score with Boots. He learned his lesson." Spur watched as her blouse came open to reveal surging breasts that had large brown areolas and pink tipped nipples that had flared and surged to erection.

She dropped her blouse on the floor and walked toward him.

"Once or twice or three times, Spur. Whatever you like. Wherever you want to put it. I'm a farm girl, we learn about sex early from watching the animals, dogs first."

Boots groaned and looked away.

"Dallman, you get your eyes looking this way again!" Martha bellowed. "You watch, damnit, like I told you to!"

She stood directly in front of Spur, so close her nipples almost touched his chest.

"This isn't necessary, Mrs. Dallman. He promised me he's never going to drink again. I'm sure you can keep him home. You're a beautiful woman, and obviously can satisfy a man . . . ."

Her hand reached down and began massaging his crotch, then the long lump that appeared by magic behind the fly of his denim pants.

"My, my, for saying no, you sure didn't instruct your big boy here not to get ready for action."

"Mrs. Dallman, this isn't necessary."

"You think I'm ugly."

"No, not at all."

"You think my titties are too small."

"They are beautiful."

"Then show me."

She unbuttoned his fly, loosened his belt and tried to pull down his pants. He stopped her.

In one quick move she loosened her skirt. It fell to the floor and just as fast she pulled down soft white underwear and stood in front of him naked. Her legs were slender and long, ending in a bush of brown hair. Her hips were full, waist narrowed and then her breasts surged out.

She caught his hand and knelt on the floor, tugging Spur with her. Then she lay on her back, spread her legs and pulled him down on top of her.

She had his pants pushed down now and pulled his turgid penis from white underpants.

"Yes, big boy, I knew you would be a huge one. Look, Boots, look what a fantastic prick McCoy has!"

Boots groaned where he sat with his coffee.

They lay on the bare wooden floor.

"It is what he needs," Martha said softly. "One last humiliation and I can cure him of going into town and getting wild drunk. Now is the time."

"This is strange, Martha. He's watching!"

"He better be!" She lifted her knees and pulled him forward. He felt his lance touch the wetness that was waiting for him.

"Hell, why not?" Spur said softly, then massaged her breasts. He saw her smile, then he eased forward and when he was inside rammed hard until he jolted forward sliding into her all the way to his pelvic bones.

She moaned softly in acceptance.

"Beautiful," she whispered in his ear. "Just marvelous. I knew you would be a good fucker. I need to talk dirty when I'm getting poked. I work better that way."

Her hips began to grind under him and set up a rhythm and soon Spur was moving to her tune. He bent and chewed on her breasts still large even though they had flattened as she lay on her back. Her legs came around his back, then lifted again and lay on his shoulders. She was almost standing on her shoulders and Spur gunned into her.

"Yes!" she said, then she climaxed. Her body shook and she wailed. A moment later he did the same thing. After fifteen of the same soft climaxes, she screamed at the top of her lungs and her hips rose to smash into his five times, then she fainted.

Spur looked at Boots.

"Don't worry. She does that when it's very good for her. She will be all right in a minute or two."

Spur stopped thrusting, then she came to and her hips pounded his and he responded and climaxed almost at once. She pushed him up and off her, gathered up her clothes and hurried into the other room.

Spur shook his head, pulled up his pants and buttoned his fly. He had not even taken off his clothes.

Martha was back a moment later, dressed and combing her soft brown hair.

"Mr. McCoy, I don't imagine you'll be around town much longer, but if you are, this never happened. Only Boots is to remember it. And if he gets a wild hair up his ass and wants to go to town to try out a new bimbo, he will be reminded what I will do if he does. And I'll make him watch me fucking one of our neighbors."

She smiled. "Between us, I think we've taught Mr. Boots Dallman two lessons in one day."

Spur grinned. "You very well may be right. I'll be happy if he never lynches anyone again."

"You can be damn sure of that!" Boots said. "I thought I was going to die out there today. That I'll remember for the rest of my life. It's not much fun facing what I did today." He looked at his wife, then reached out and petted her breasts through the green blouse.

"As for you, I'll save all my fucking for you. Twice a week, at least."

"Hey, every night if you want. I'm here and ready."

Spur saw Boots' hand vanish inside her blouse and saw the light sparkle in her eyes. Spur faded out the door. For Boots, one of the worst days in his life was going to start getting a lot better quickly.

Spur walked back to his horse, mounted and rode away. He took one last look at Boots Dallman's ranch and farm and wished him well.

16

On his way into town, Spur rode past the laundry. He grinned and moved up to the hitching rail and tied his mare, then went inside. At first he thought the place was empty.

"Just about to close up," a voice called. "State your business." It was a woman.

"Came to pick up some laundry," Spur called.

A fluff of brown hair showed from behind a stack of boxes, then deep green eyes peered out.

"Oh, hi!" the owner of the voice came out from the stack of boxes and grinned. It was the same girl who had taken in his laundry that morning. "Decided to come back after all?"

"Figures as how. My laundry ready?"

"Almost. I'll finish it, only be a minute. Would you mind snapping that spring night lock and throwing the bolt for me so nobody else will come? We start so early in the morning we usually close early as well."

Spur locked the door and slid the bolt home, then

stood at the counter waiting.

"Could you give me a hand?" the girl asked. "Right back here."

Spur grinned and went around the end of the counter and through the baskets and trays to where the voice came from.

She stood at a work table, and had just tied up a bundle of wash in white paper. She knotted the string, snapped it in half, then handed the package to him.

Her eyes widened as he took it, brushing his hand against hers.

"Oh, say, I was wondering . . ." She frowned, looked away, then sighed and looked back. "Oh, forget it."

Spur let a small smile slide onto his face. "What were you wondering? I'm in no big hurry. What's bothering you?"

She turned back, eyes snapping, a dimple on her right cheek. She brushed at long brown hair that had straggled over one eye.

"Well, I was wondering if you could give me some advice. You're a stranger but I feel I could trust you."

"Advice is cheap."

"But I need some—please?" She reached out and touched his arm, then drew her hand back quickly.

"About this morning, that three dollars and dinner. That was just talk. I was feeling all squirmy and hot and I just said things I shouldn't."

"I understand."

She motioned with one hand. "Come back here so we can talk."

They moved through the back part of the store to a sectioned-off area that were apparently living quarters. Two rooms were furnished, a bedroom and small kitchen. A window looked out on the alley.

"Home," she said simply. "Oh—I'm Sue, and I'm eighteen and I'm just all mixed up."

"I'm Spur McCoy," he said.

She waved him into a straight-backed chair near a small table and she sat in a second chair.

"I tell everyone I'm twenty-one and an orphan. Not true. I got folks. They live in Portland, but I ran away. Was that wrong?"

Spur watched her. She was serious. "It just depends on why you ran away, and what you've done since. Why did you leave your parents' home?"

"I was sixteen, and my daddy drank a lot, and Momma was sickly, she had the fever. Days at a time she barely woke up. So I had to do the chores and cooking. Daddy liked to hug me, and one day he hugged and hugged and then his hips started pushing and pumping against mine. He was *doing* it. He stops and tells me to lay down on my bed and lifts up my skirt and then he undresses me.

"I was so scared I couldn't even talk. When I was all bare he made me undress him, and I was trembling and scared and excited. I'd never seen a man's . . . thing . . . before. It was so big!

"Then he was naked and he grabbed it with his hand and began pumping back and forth with one hand and rubbing my breasts with the other. I was still scared but it felt kind of good, all warm and wanting him to rub and rub. Then he just spurted all over me and he grunted and grabbed his clothes and left.

"The next night he came in and did the same thing. About a week later he started playing with me and pushing his finger into me, and then in another week, he was doing it, right inside me.

"I tried to make him stop, 'cause I knew it was

bad. But he wouldn't stop. I locked my door and he broke it down. He made me do terrible things to him and for him. I decided I could either kill him or run away. I didn't know how to kill him, so I took all the money I could find in his wallet one night when he was drunk, and got a stage ticket to Boise, and then came down here."

She looked up at him, her big green eyes still serious. "I been here almost two years working in this laundry, and now the owner lets me stay in back here and watch the place. Did I do wrong running away?"

"No, Sue, of course not. Your father was the wrong one."

"Yeah, I thought of that. But somehow it never mattered much to me when he did it to me. I didn't mind. I finally learned to get a little excited myself. The advice I want is this. Since I don't mind it, should I be a fancy woman in a saloon and make six or eight dollars a night? That's a lot of money, maybe two hundred dollars a month! I get fifteen dollars a month and my room here."

"Well, Sue, that's a decision you'll have to make. Is there anything else you think you might like doing? Like teaching school or getting married?"

She laughed. "Oh, yes, I wanted to get married. But that will just kind of happen. I don't talk or write good enough to teach school."

"Sue, the best advice I can give you is that you should do exactly what you want to do. Life is short, in spite of what you might think at eighteen. So don't waste life, live it. Do what you want to do— and of course be prepared for any consequences."

"Like fancy women when they get diseases and pregnant and things like that?"

"Yes, and they sometimes get beat up, and every now and then one of the whores get killed."

"Heaven protect us!" She watched him a minute. "Yes, thank you, I have decided." She stood and moved to the stove, making a fire. "Now, I promised you supper, so I had better make you something to eat. How about some fried potatoes and onions mixed up with some chopped up bacon? My daddy always liked that."

Spur said that would be fine and watched her work over the small sink and the stove. She chattered on, about Portland, about how much it rained, how you could count on rain every single day during winter.

"Then if it didn't rain, you could run and sing and jump and be so happy because it wasn't raining! But I really liked Portland. Maybe I'll go back there sometime after daddy dies. He's getting old. I bet he's over forty-five now!"

The fried potatoes were delightful. She served them with biscuits and homemade jam and hot coffee and some fresh peas.

"Best meal I've had in a week," Spur said.

She smiled and poured him more coffee, then sat and stared at him.

"You are the most handsome man that I've ever cooked supper for," she said. It was an honest, straight statement. "I guess you're about the prettiest man I've ever seen!" Sue came and stood in front of where he sat. "You have helped me make up my mind. I am going to try to better myself. I got past the eighth grade, but not much farther. If I work on my numbers, I bet I could be a clerk in one of the mercantiles. That would be a step up. Hoffer's has all that nice household merchandise. But the women don't like to go in there and have him wait on them. They think he's weird. Maybe I could work for him.''

As she talked she leaned forward, her white peasant blouse billowed forward as it had in the store.

"I also believe in paying my debts. You helped me, now I will give you the only thing I have you might want.''

Spur looked down her blouse at her big breasts.

"Sue, you don't have to do this.''

"I know, but I want to. I don't jump in bed with just any man I see." She caught the bottom of the blouse and slid it off over her head.

Her breasts jiggled from the motion and Spur sucked in his breath. Twin peaks thrust out at him, the nipples extended by hot, pulsating blood. The large pink areolas over cream white flesh were begging to be kissed.

"Mr. McCoy," she said, her eyes half closed. "I would be ever so grateful if you would kiss me now.''

He leaned forward and kissed her soft lips. Her arms went around him and her breasts crushed against him. Her tongue darted into his mouth at once and he could feel her hips thrusting against his.

She let the kiss last a long time, then leaned back and looked up at him.

"Everytime I kiss someone I think it gets better and better. Why is that, Mr. McCoy?''

"Because you only kiss when you're sexually excited, and that increases your excitement, and mine, and it seems like you want those feelings to go on forever and ever.''

Her face brightened. "Yes!" Then she kissed him again. Her slender body pressed against him from knee to chest now and he had to suck in a quick breath. He was surprised by the heat of her body through the cloth.

When the second kiss ended, she caught his hand and moved it to her breasts.

"Rub them, pet them for me," she whispered, an urgency in her voice he had not heard before.

His hand massaged one mound, then the other, and her breathing became a panting, her mouth opened and her eyes closed and her hands massaged his back and then his chest. Slowly she opened the buttons on his shirt and one hand snaked inside, rubbing his chest, toying with his chest hair.

"I'm going to fall over unless we lay down somewhere!" she said. She took his hand and led him into the small bedroom with its single bed covered by a quilted comforter done in the double wedding ring design.

She sat on the edge of the bed and motioned him to sit beside her.

She stared into his eyes, her deep green orbs now serious and determined.

"I am not going to become a whore, and I won't even joke about it anymore, the way I did to you. I promise never, never again to let anyone see my titties like I did today, and I'll always wear a chemise and a wrapper so they won't look so big. There, that will be a good start."

"I should think so," Spur said. He reached down and kissed her. She was as eager and enthused as ever, and slowly pushed him down on his back so she could lie on top of him.

Spur realized it had been weeks since he had taken on two different women the same day. Mentally he shrugged; he took life as it came to him, there was no sense fighting it.

She took his shirt off, then his boots, and then her

own long skirt. She had on only knee-length drawers. Her breasts bounded and jolted around, to Spur's immense delight.

When she pulled down his pants and his underwear, Sue gasped. His staff was at full erection and ready to perform.

"Golly whee!" Sue said. "Golly whee! I've never seen anything like that before. It's huge!"

"The better to love you," Spur said and she let him unfasten the drawstring on the drawers and pull them down.

She stopped him and pushed him back on the bed and sat on his stomach, then lowered her breasts to his mouth. She smiled at the look of satisfaction on his face.

"I thought you would like to chew on me. Men just seem to enjoy it. I climaxed the first time. Now I'm a little slower. Oh, I might yell if I really get excited, don't be surprised."

For the next fifteen minutes, several things she did surprised him, but he had some new ideas for her as well, and she kissed him one last time, then nodded.

"Yes, please, Mr. Spur McCoy, I really wish that you would fuck me now, fast and hard before I just explode!"

The second time she insisted they do it standing up. She leaned against the wall and locked her legs behind his back. To Spur's pleasure it worked delightfully well. They laughed and the second time Sue cried as she climaxed, and then they rested side by side on the bed.

She touched his shoulder and looked at her.

"I am going to start dressing better, and I'm going to try to get a better job. Yes, I definitely do want to get married and have babies. Three, I guess,

two boys and a girl. That would be about right." She
rolled over and held her chin in her hands and stared
at him, her fingers twirling the hairs on his chest.

"You want to marry me? We're good fucking
together."

Spur chuckled. "I'm afraid I'm a traveling man.
I'll be gone from here in two or three days."

"Oh. You don't like me."

He kissed her nose, then her cheek, then her lips.
"I *do* like you. You are a wonderful, bouncy, smart,
ambitious girl. But I have to move on." He looked at
his watch. It was almost six-thirty. He had another
job to do before the night was over. He had to get
the principals in the counterfeiting game to show
their hand.

17

The time was nearly four P.M. when Spur rode back into town and tied his horse in back of the hotel. He went up to his room for some supplies. The drama was nearing an end and he might have to leave town quickly. He took his Spencer repeating rifle and an extra box of rounds, along with two loaded tubes and put them in the boot on the saddle.

In his saddlebags he put an extra shirt and a pair of jeans, then packed in some store bought jerky and dried fruit. He put the horse in the small hotel stable behind the hotel and knew it would be safe there.

He washed up, changed his shirt and put on a clean neckerchief to keep his throat bandage clean. He could turn his head anyway he wanted to now with little pain. It must be healing. His leg gave him no trouble at all now.

Spur checked his boots. The heel on one was loose. He dug out the spare pair of boots he had picked up in Denver. They had a feature built into the heel

163

that had fascinated him. On the right boot, there was a small trigger in the hollow just in front of the heel. By pushing the button, a two inch knife slid out from the side of the heel leather. He had sharpened it to razor proportions.

Spur tried the device, then pressed the button again and carefully pushed the blade back until it locked. It could come in handy sometime. He put on the new boots and was ready to go.

Spur walked out of the hotel with his .45 riding low on his right hip, crossed the street and angled for the second floor office of lawyer Kane Turner. It was time to tighten up the set screws and let Turner know he was under suspicion.

McCoy went in without knocking and found Kane working on some papers on his desk. He looked up, his brow creasing with a frown. Hoffer probably had talked with Kane, telling him that Spur was on to them, or at least knew about Hoffer and the printer.

"Yes, Mr. McCoy. I haven't heard a thing from the sheriff about that shooting. I'd guess you won't be charged. Hell, you were a witness not a suspect."

"Never can tell in a strange town, Mr. Turner. I'm glad to hear the news. Trouble is, now I have a new problem."

Kane stood. Spur saw no weapon, but he could have a hideout somewhere within reaching distance.

"Yeah, counselor, seems like somebody pawned off some bogus money on me. Look at this." Spur tossed an envelope on the lawyer's desk. It held three new, virgin, unfolded twenty dollar bills. They were from the counterfeit supply Turner's wife had given to Spur.

"Look good to me. Bank gets new bills from time to time. What's wrong with them?"

"You know what's wrong, Turner. You've been

watching the work on the plates and the press for the last two or three months. All the serial numbers are identical. It's the first thing to check for on a batch of counterfeit bills."

Kane never looked at the money.

"And you're saying I had something to do with this counterfeiting?"

"Damn right, Kane, you, the artist and engraving man, Hoffer, and the printer Wintergarden who Hoffer shot dead. Last night you went to see Hoffer just after I told you about the killing. You wanted to be sure Hoffer had done it."

Kane smiled. "Afraid you'll need more evidence than that to make it stand up in our circuit rider courtroom, Mr. McCoy. Proof is what the judge looks for."

"I've got a million dollars worth of proof," McCoy said. He drew his .45 so quickly that Kane could only stare at it.

"There is no need for firearms, I'm a peaceful man, and I uphold the law."

"The ones you want to," Spur said.

"I can prove I had nothing to do with those counterfeit bills. I have a document in my desk drawer."

"Get it."

Kane bent toward the drawer, then drew a derringer from his inner coat pocket and fired a shot blindly toward Spur. If it had been bird shot it could have blinded Spur. As it was the solid lead slug from the .45 derringer slammed past Spur's left ear, buzzing as it flew past and stuck in the plastered walls.

Spur lunged away and fired, digging a .45 round into Kane's right shoulder before he could get off a second shot. The small weapon fell from Kane's hand as he jolted backward against the wall. His left hand held his bleeding shoulder.

"If you get in the first shot, never miss. Think about that when you're in prison on counterfeiting charges."

"Get me to Doc Rawson! I'll bleed to death."

"Good, save the county and state some money. You show me where you hid the engraved plates for those twenty dollar bills and I'll carry you to the Doc's office."

"I don't know what you're talking about."

"Then why did you try to kill me just now?"

"You were threatening me with a gun. I have a right to defend myself with deadly force."

"True." Spur searched the man, found no other weapon and pushed him into a chair. "Stay there until I finish tearing this place apart."

"Why?"

"I figure you have something near a half million dollars around here somewhere in twenties. Want to tell me where you hid them?"

"Ridiculous!" Kane said, but his frown deepened. He used his handkerchief to push inside his shirt to try to slow down the bleeding.

Spur jerked open drawers, dumped out two on the desk top. When he pulled out the wide drawer in the center of the desk, it stuck. Underneath it he found a box fastened to the bottom of the drawer. In the box were stacks of twenty dollar bills. There were ten packets.

"Twenty thousand dollars worth," Spur said. "That's a start, now where is the rest?"

"Bastard! I'm still bleeding!"

"So suffer a little." Spur kept looking. In a locked file which he broke open he found trust deeds and legal descriptions and property deeds to town property. Most were dated within a two month period. He guessed the property had been purchased somehow with the bogus money, so the sales were invalid. He set them aside, and went back to dumping drawers.

No more money.

Spur moved to the small storage closet. Three boxes on a shelf were marked, "Old records 1872." One of the boxes looked newer than the others and had been marked with a different kind of pen making a wide line. He pulled the box off the shelf and opened it. The box was full of packets of twenty dollar bills, all with identical serial numbers.

"Don't know a thing about this either, I'd guess," Spur said looking up at Kane Turner.

The lawyer scowled. "Get me a doctor!"

"The doctors in prison aren't much good, but you have a month or two in jail here before you head to a federal lockup. You might even live."

"I don't know a thing about any counterfeiting," Turner said. "I do keep records for some of my clients. Somebody else put those there. Planted them on me to get me in trouble. It's all circumstantial. You have no proof that I did anything wrong. And you shot me. I'll charge you with attempted murder."

"You're a dreamer, Kane."

Spur heard something behind him and whirled, but there wasn't time. A .44 roared behind him and he felt the pain as a bullet grazed his left shoulder as he went down to one knee. He had no chance for a shot. He couldn't even see his attacker.

"Sloppy, McCoy, damned sloppy police work," a voice said behind him. "You want to live more than a few seconds, ease your hogsleg onto the floor and lay down flat on your belly."

Spur had no choice. He did as he was told. It had to be Hoffer. Sounded lilke his voice. Spur turned and looked.

"Good evening, Mr. McCoy," Hoffer said, the .44 six-gun aimed at Spur's head. "Nice that you could come along on our little trip."

"Josh, get me to a doctor. I'm bleeding like a stuck hog."

"Yes indeed, Kane, right soon. Get your half of the twenties first and wrap them for traveling."

"Travel . . ."

"Right. We can't stay here anymore. McCoy here has probably been working with the sheriff. We've got too much to lose."

Kane helped as they wrapped the box of money with twine, then Turner held the gun on McCoy as they went down to the street by the back stairs. Hoffer put the big box into the back of a surrey beside another one the same size.

"Only rig I've ever seen worth a million dollars," Hoffer said. "Come on, Kane, smile damnit! We're getting out of here clean and taking our little witness along."

"First the doctor!" Turner shrieked.

"Yes, Yes." Hoffer took rawhide from his pocket and tied Spur's wrists together in front of his chest, then ordered him into the rear seat of the surrey.

They drove to Doc Rawson's office. Turner went in by himself and Hoffer watched Spur.

"Never work," Spur said.

"I've got plans," Hoffer said. "I don't like to be pushed around, by anybody. You made a mistake there. I've been working it all out."

"Everybody will be watching for those bogus bills now, in all the states and territories."

Hoffer mopped his brow with a kerchief. "Not rightly possible, because nobody will know about them. You ain't gonna tell nobody nothing about them."

"Only one way to make that work."

"Right, you guessed it, big man. Only this time I make sure the damn hangman's knot is tied right. Got a couple of old timers to make it for me, to tie it right. Guess where the rope is, McCoy, you damned fool? You think I was gonna sit by and let you come in here and threaten me like that? Not a chance."

"You kill me and there'll be twenty federal lawmen in here within two weeks."

"Fine, we won't be anywhere around. They won't never find us, not in a million years." Hoffer chuckled and the nervous tick over his right eye began pulsating again. "Might say we have a million reasons they won't find us." He laughed again.

Spur tried to get the rawhide undone. Hoffer had tied him the right way, one strand and strong knots, no chance to stretch the rawhide. At least his feet were free. He leaned against the boxes holding the counterfeit. He'd never had a million dollar pillow before.

Spur also had to make certain, somehow, that he didn't have a pair of millionaires as his executioner and grave digger.

It was nearly a half hour later when Kane Turner came out of the doctor's office. He carried his jacket and his shirt sleeve was empty, his arm in a sling across his chest.

Turner got into the rig and Hoffer drove away.

"Looks like you'll live," Hoffer said.

"Cut up my shoulder bad. Doc said I shouldn't

even move it for two weeks."

"He always says that. Makes the old fart feel important."

"What now?"

"We go past your place so you can pack a bag of traveling clothes. I got everything I need."

"What about him?" Turner said pointing at Spur.

"Hell, he ain't gonna need much, and he won't eat nothing at all." Hoffer laughed. "I owe that bastard one for threatening me yesterday. Now let's get to your place. Don't bother with your old woman. Just pack some clothes and a couple of six-guns if you got them, and let's get moving."

Spur McCoy narrowed his eyes a little as he considered his situation. Hoffer wanted to hang him, and this time he was sure the fat little man would do it right with a few .44 slugs to make certain. Hoffer wouldn't let him live through the night, that was certain.

Spur had to figure some way to get free and get the jump on Hoffer, before they stopped the rig for the execution if possible.

Damn, getting hung once was plenty. Spur had no desire to be the guest of honor at another hanging.

18

At the Turner house, Hoffer grabbed the lawyer's sleeve before he stepped down.

"I'll give you five minutes, no more. If you're not here in five minutes I'm leaving. Make sure you're here." Hoffer took out a gold watch, popped open the face and read the time. In five minutes it would be dusk. Spur watched Turner go up to his back door and inside. They sat parked in the alley waiting.

Hoffer turned and watched Spur.

"Hear you're some kind of a lawman. Tough turnips! Just one less lawman to worry about. I ain't never been too fond of your type anyway. This is just frosting on the cake for me." He laughed softly and Spur saw his small, close set green eyes darken.

"Damn! but I am gonna enjoy hanging you again. Not many men can brag that they've personally hung the same man twice! Yes sir, I'll have a story to tell!"

Hoffer checked his watch, then put it away.

"Hurry up, lawyer! I ain't got all night to sit here and wait for you. Fact is, if I left now, I'd be twice as rich. A damn fine idea to consider!"

Spur looked down at his boots—and remembered, he had on the new pair, the ones with the knife in the heel! Now he watched the sky darken. When it was dark enough he could pull his right leg up and push the trigger, then it would be a matter of seconds before his hands would be free!

Before he could build a plan, Turner came out the back door, ran to the buggy and pushed a large carpetbag in back next to the boxes of money and beside Spur.

"Let's go!" Turner said.

The whip cracked over the back of the black mare and she stepped out smartly.

Spur knew he would have a better chance if he could get free before they left town. The problem was it wasn't quite dark enough yet, and when he tried to move his right boot, he found his foot wedged under the carpetbag.

"Boise?" Turner asked, "then on to San Francisco. What do you think of that plan? We could pass plenty of the twenties in Frisco."

"Might be worth considering. First we have our necktie party. I want you to watch Spur so he don't get feisty back there. Be a damn shame to have to shoot him and miss a hanging."

Spur could see Turner shaking his head. "I don't know if it's such a good idea to kill a lawman, especially a United States lawman. They are going to do a search." Turner shifted his position so he could see Spur.

"So what? We'll be out of the state by the time they know about it." Hoffer turned and grinned at

Spur. "How does it feel to hear us talking about killing your ass?"

"Like listening to a pair of crazy men talking," Spur said.

Hoffer slammed the handle of the buggy whip at Spur, but only grazed him on the shoulder. It was the same one where the derringer bullet had left a bloody crease. Spur grimaced and settled lower in the back seat of the surrey.

Five minutes later it was fully dark, but they had left the last houses at the edge of town as well. They were heading west along the river road, downstream toward Boise. That was a hundred and forty-five mile ride. Spur knew he would never last that long.

For an hour they drove along. Turner kept looking over the back seat at Spur, and even in the dark he was so close he could tell if Spur tried to cut free his hands. Spur knew he had to wait.

They came to occasional trees along the road, and once the stage trail dipped closer to the river and went through a heavy patch of woods, but Hoffer kept shaking his head. "We got to find exactly the right limb for this sucker to swing from."

Turner appeared to be tiring of his turned position, and gradually he edged back more forward. Soon his back was to Spur and it was time!

Spur edged his leg out from under the carpetbag and with his left hand pulled his right boot up on his left leg. He watched the two in the front seat but they were talking softly about something. He pushed the small trigger in front of the boot heel and saw the glint of the blade. Carefully he placed his bound wrists next to the blade, adjusted, then moved them again until the blade touched the rawhide.

Then he sawed back and forth with his wrists.

The blade bit into his flesh and he could feel the warm blood dripping. He looked again in the dimness of the bad light and adjusted his wrists and sawed again.

Hoffer turned and looked at Spur.

"You care what kind of a tree I use to hang you from, McCoy?" Hoffer laughed. "Be poetic if it was another oak tree, but we'll probably have to settle for a maple, or maybe even a pine or a fir. Going to get farther away from town, so just rest yourself. You try anything funny and you get gut shot. That way you'll live for an hour or so and we can still hang you!" Hoffer laughed again and whacked the reins against the mare who picked up the pace a little.

Spur had not moved while Hoffer talked to him. Now he tried again, slicing harder, faster with the razor sharp blade. He felt one strand part, then the second and his hands came apart. He pushed the blade back in place.

Cautiously and with no sound he opened the carpetbag, hoping against hope that Turner had put an extra six gun in it. His hands explored the bag silently, no gun.

He took out a heavy wool sweater and considered it. It was the pullover type and would work for one. He checked the surrey. It was the open kind with a roof but no side curtains of any kind. The buggy whip rode in its holder fastened on the left side of the driver's seat for easy access by the driver.

It also was within easy reach for Spur. He held the sweater in his lap with the opening spread and waited. Then he reached carefully forward and lifted the whip out of its holder without a sound.

He was ready. Spur put the whip across his lap, picked up the sweater and in one swift movement, leaned over the front seat, jerked the open part of the sweater downward over Kane Turner's head and at the same time, pushed him so he toppled out of the open side of the surrey.

Without a wasted move Spur grabbed the thin leather end of the buggy whip, threw it around Hoffer's head, then pulled both ends backward sharply choking the killer with his own whip.

Turner screamed as he fell out of the surrey in his blinded condition and hit the roadway hard.

Spur shouted at the horse to giddap and at the same time pulled the leather whip tighter and tighter around Hoffer's neck.

Then Hoffer did something Spur had not anticipated. He surged backwards, both hands over his head, grasping, clawing for Spur's face or head. One of his hands caught Spur's bandage around his throat and he yanked forward, half tearing the bandage away, sending waves of pain through Spur. In his agony Spur dropped the whip, tore Hoffer's hands from his neck, and jumped out of the rig.

He hit on the rutted dirt of the trail, rolled once and sprang to his feet, running at right angles to the roadway and the surrey. Here they were a mile from the river, but each valley held scatterings of pine, fir and heavy underbrush.

Spur charged for the dark shapes of the trees maybe two hundred yards ahead. He heard Hoffer shouting behind him. A pistol cracked twice, but Hoffer had no idea which direction Spur had run in the solid darkness. The shots went wild.

McCoy kept running. He heard the men talking behind him. Hoffer screaming that of course they had to find him. He would expose their whole scheme. Everything was ruined if Spur got away.

Spur stopped running and listened. They stopped

shouting but some of the words still came through.

They would stop there for the night, and find him in the morning. Take turns sleeping in the rig. No fire, that would bring him back.

Yes, they would keep their guns ready!

Spur sat on the ground and took stock. He felt the bandage and did what he could to get it back in position to cover his aching throat. Doc Rawson would be furious. Still it was better than testing another hangman's noose.

He looked back and could hear sounds as the pair began getting ready to spend the night. The horse was unhitched. Spur grinned. That was their first mistake.

Neither of them seemed to be an outdoorsman. Both had spent most of their time indoors, in court or in a store. He would have the advantage here.

What he needed was a gun. Could he slip up on them, knock out or kill the one awake silently, and get his gun?

The odds were not on his side.

If he tried and failed, he was a dead man.

Another idea was needed. Spur continued to the woods. He had checked his pockets and found nothing useful, not even a pen knife. He had no sheath knife on his belt. The only blade he had was on his boot. He sat down and triggered it into place, then tried to detach it. He could not see well enough to figure it out. Spur found a double fist sized rock, put his heel on the ground and broke the blade off his boot. It was an inch and a half long, but sharp.

An hour later, Spur had made two spears, not very straight, but sharpened to needle points. He spent another two hours scouting a good spot to ambush the pair. They would move together to protect each other.

A pit would be good if he had a shovel.

His Spencer repeating rifle would be better.

Spur quit dreaming.

They were about ten miles from town. He could start walking now and get to Twin Falls by morning. But only if one of them had gone down the trail toward town to watch for him. Both men could shoot. He would be dead a mile down the road.

The second obvious solution was to disable the horse and put the men on foot. That way he would have the advantage.

Or disable the surrey.

Well before dawn, Spur decided the horse had to be put down. He had made four more spears. The best was six feet long and sharp as a pencil point. He went back to the stage road and left a trail in the dust that even Hoffer should be able to follow. It went back toward town.

After a quarter of a mile the stage road went through an arm of the wooded area. Trees and brush grew close on both sides. Spur spent another hour dragging logs and brush and downed limbs into the middle of the road to make a barricade. It was just around a corner so the driver would have no chance to see it before he had to stop.

Spur picked his attack point carefully, then screened it from the roadway with more broken brush so neither man on the rig could see him until it was too late.

Spur sat against a tree then and went to sleep. Each time he slept four or five minutes he would fall away from the tree and wake up.

He stayed awake the last time he came to and found the sun just coming up.

McCoy checked his spears and his retreat plan, then climbed a friendly fir tree and looked down the trail toward Boise.

He saw one man on the stage road, and it was obvious that he had found Spur's tracks. Soon the surrey joined him and both men rode toward the trap.

Spur went down the tree, positioned himself behind his blind and waited.

He could hear the jingle of the harness and the singletree long before he saw the surrey. The sounds came closer and then the rig came around the bend in the trail.

Spur had positioned himself at the point where the rig probably would stop after Hoffer saw the brush pile. The horse was just across from him now.

Spur leaped out of the blind, with the six foot long and inch and a half diameter spear poised and ran forward with it like a lance, and point aimed directly at the mare's heaving side.

Hoffer saw him and shouted. Turner swept around with his pistol, but hit the roof supports and swore. Hoffer tried to get his six-gun up, but he was too late.

Spur lunged forward with the spear, driving it all the way through the animal, smashing one rib, separating another on the far side, tearing through vital organs.

The Secret Agent darted around the front of the horse and bolted into the deep brush five feet away on the far side of the roadway. Hoffer got off one shot that went high. Turner never did fire. He had banged his wounded shoulder and screamed in agony.

Once outside the covering trees, Spur stopped and peered back at the horse. The mare screamed in mortal pain and he heard her going down, thrashing on the ground in the harness and the traces. She screamed again, a nerve jangling sound, but it cut off suddenly with the report of a pistol shot.

·Then all was quiet.

"Now, you sons of bitches, I'm coming to get you," Spur said quietly.

Spur found a point where he could watch the pair of tenderfoots as he peered around a fir tree so they could not see him. They opened the boxes of money and held it, threw it down and stormed around. He could not hear what they said. They found a small shovel on the surrey and tried to bury the money. Both gave up long before they had a hole deep enough.

At last they stuffed their carpetbags with as many of the stacks of bills as they could carry and began walking down the stage road toward Boise.

As he waited, Spur had worked on constructing a bow. He had found a flexible piece of maple and tried it. Not the best, but with the laces from his boot he had a serviceable bowstring. Then he found willow and cut some arrows that would be enough to scare the pair. He had to drive them away from the stage road, and any chance of them catching the stage heading for Boise.

Spur cut back to the stage road three miles ahead. He was forward of the heavily loaded pair. He found his spot. The road followed a narrow valley that passed near a sharp cliff. Spur went to the top of the sixty foot dropoff and gathered a dozen, fifty pound boulders. Then he sat down and sharpened six more arrows and waited. He had no feathers or any way to attach them. The rocks might be more effective.

A half hour later he spotted the counterfeiting pair coming along the road. They were moving slow, dragging along, the paper money much heavier now than when they had packed it in the carpetbags.

They found the cut and moved at once to the shady side, right under where Spur lay above.

He readied four of the boulders, placing them on the brink of the cliff, then pushed them over as quickly as he could. All four thundered down, hitting the cliff, knocking loose more rocks and sand. Hoffer heard them coming and darted out of the way.

Turner was slower. He lifted up, tried to push with his shot up arm and it folded. One of the fifty pound rocks caught him squarely on the left knee and smashed it, dropping him to the ground where a dozen other smaller rocks hit him as they raced past.

Turner screamed at Hoffer to help him. Hoffer looked up at the cliff and shook his head.

"Only one way you can help me now, asshole," he said. "That is not to slow me down." Hoffer ran back toward Turner, then looked up and saw two more rocks coming. Hoffer stood and aimed carefully with his pistol. He fired four times. Three of the rounds hit Kane Turner in the chest, slashing through his heart and lungs, killing him instantly.

"Now it's all mine!" Hoffer screamed. "I'm a millionaire!"

Spur shot one arrow at him. It went straight for a ways, then slanted to the left and tumbled to the ground. Spur knew he would have to do a lot more work on the arrows so they would function without feathers. He needed to lighten the tails because he could not make the points heavier.

Hoffer put two shots into the top of the cliff and reloaded.

"You're a dead man, Spur McCoy. You just don't know it yet. I'm no tenderfoot out here, and remember I have the guns. He ran forward toward Turner's body, but turned back. Spur kept dropping more rocks at the right time to keep Hoffer away. Turner must have a weapon! Spur wanted it.

After ten minutes, Hoffer shot twice more at Spur, then threw out half of the stacks of bills, and began to run down the stage road toward Boise. Now it looked like he would take the stage no matter which way it was headed.

When Spur was sure Hoffer was gone, he worked around to the side of the cliff and went down. He checked Turner's body and found a well worn .44, a holster and a gunbelt with another twenty rounds. Spur stripped the gun belt off the dead man, went through his pockets and found a pen knife, but little else of value. He strapped the gun belt on, discarding his useless one with the .45 rounds in it.

"Now, Hoffer, the odds are evened up just a little bit. I'm coming to nail your carcass, and then hang you!"

19

His big fist hefted the six-gun, slid it into leather, then pulled it out and aimed. He did that five times, each time getting a little faster, more familiar with the new weapon.

The iron had a different feel to it, a different balance than the Colt .45 Spur usually carried—but any hogleg in a storm.

He took one more look at Kane Turner, then jogged in the general direction Josh Hoffer had taken. He left the road that made only a scratch on the surface of the bold Idaho land, and worked his way up to an open spot. From the height he could see three miles in both directions along the stage road.

Far to the right, heading west, he saw a solitary figure moving steadily along the road. Hoffer.

Walking. How far would he go before he elected to wait for the stage?

Spur looked to the west. At the far end of his view of the road he saw a thin trail of dust rising into the

sky. He waited a moment more and knew the rig
was coming toward him.

The stage from Boise heading for Twin Falls!

Without consciously making the decision, Spur
ran downhill. He moved at an angle to cut off Hoffer
before the stage arrived. Could he do it?

Spur slowed his charge down the hill, held onto
the flapping holster and resumed his Indian trot. A
Mescalero Apache had taught him the technique one
summer. The idea was that a man alone in the mountains or desert could outrun a man or a horse if he
knows how.

Spur learned how. The gait was faster than walking, but was not an actual run, more of a trot, with
one foot barely leaving the ground before the other
one touched. The Apaches could set a pace at six to
eight miles an hour, and keep it up for ten hours
straight.

Spur knew he could get the two miles to the stage
road, but he wasn't sure where Hoffer would be. He
couldn't have seen the stage coming yet. Spur
changed his angle so he moved slightly west, which
would put him between Hoffer and the stage. He
had another idea that just might work, no matter
where Hoffer was hiding.

The first mile went easily, with Spur breaking a
sweat after the first ten minutes. He was closer now,
and could not see the spiral of dust over the slight
rise in the stage road. For that he was thankful
because Hoffer couldn't see it either.

He ran, sticking as close to six miles an hour as he
could, and when he looked up at the stage trail the
next time, he saw the dust, and a black dot moving
toward him.

Five minutes later he came to the road and
checked to the east, but Hoffer was not in sight.

There was no chance that Hoffer was west of Spur, so the plan would work.

He dragged the remains of a downed fir tree across the trail. The tree was only four inches in diameter and twenty feet tall. It would not even slow down a charging stage coach. And Spur intended for it to be charging. He picked his spot near a pair of man-sized boulders, and checked the six-gun. It held four rounds. He put two more in and let the hammer down carefully.

Spur stayed out of sight as the coach came closer. Then as the rig rolled within fifty yards, it started to slow when it saw the tree across the main track. There was plenty of room on either side to drive around it in this flat, open country.

About the time the driver decided to go around the tree, Spur jumped up and charged the stage, his six-gun out. He fired two shots in the air, and when the driver looked in his direction, fired twice more well in front of the horses. The driver hunkered down and slapped the reins on the team of six, urging them faster. A pistol cracked out the side window of the coach and Spur dove for the dirt.

He fired his last two rounds as the coach whipped past him in a swirl of dust. Spur dumped out the brass, loaded three more and fired them into the air as the coach raced away.

The Secret Service Agent grinned at the vanishing coach. The driver would be spooked enough that he wouldn't even slow down no matter who was standing beside the road trying to stop him for a ride. And what a story he would have to tell when he got to Twin Falls!

Spur walked toward Twin Falls for half a mile to a patch of woods, found himself a good observation point and settled down to wait. Hoffer would be coming along soon, he had no other choice of a place to go. The next stage would be heading for Boise, but it might not come for several hours.

An hour later Spur still waited. He decided if Hoffer didn't show up in another hour, Spur would start back-tracking him.

Josh Hoffer did not come. Spur stared down the stage road as far as he could see. There was no sign of anyone.

Spur sighed and began walking back toward where Josh Hoffer had last been seen, not much more than a half mile. When Spur came to the spot along the roadway he could see Hoffer's tracks, then where his footprints had crossed the new prints made by the horses and stage.

Spur looked up. The counterfeiter's tracks headed for a small grove of trees at the side of a ravine a quarter of a mile away. Hoffer was looking for some shade; he was not used to the burning sun and the outdoors.

A half hour later Spur edged into the trees from the side, moved cautiously toward the point nearest the stage road, and scanned the wooded area carefully.

He could not see Hoffer. Without making a sound, Spur moved up to the edge of the woods until he had checked behind every tree. Hoffer was not hiding there.

Spur creased his brow, slapped his hat against his leg to dislodge some of the dust, and went back to the open area. It took him three crossings before he found Hoffer's tracks. The tenderfoot had angled around the woods and moved into the mouth of the small canyon.

Spur eyed the area. It could be a trap with Hoffer just inside the opening of the rock sided ravine, waiting for Spur to fall into the snare. McCoy followed the tracks another hundred yards until he was sure they led into the ravine, then ran to one side and came up at the edge of the opening.

The gully was maybe fifty yards wide at the mouth, held a dry stream bed and a few spots of brush, but no real trees. The soil was sandy and rocky here and the arroyo angled into the low range of hills, bent sharply to the left and continued.

There was no ambush point near the opening. Spur walked across the entrance slowly, scanning the ground, and soon came up with the counterfeiter's bootprints. They led directly up the center of the little canyon.

Spur eyed the area critically. There was shade higher in the canyon, and there well could be a spring that fed the trees. Hoffer must be out of water and be hunting a drink. Spur could think of no other reason the fugitive would leave the stage road and wander back in the hills.

There was nothing to do but dig him out. Spur eyed the iron he carried and wished he knew more about it. But the twenty rounds he had for the .44 did not give him the luxury of sighting in the weapon.

The big U.S. Secret Service agent pushed the iron back in its leather home and watched the ground as he tracked Hoffer into the canyon. Here and there, sheet rock slanted down toward the creek, but another fifty yards ahead the ground was soft again and Spur picked up the tracks.

He had moved less than a quarter of a mile when he came to the bend and decided a small recon was in order. He should have a point man to send out, but this was a long time after the war. He peered over a boulder into this part of the canyon. It was much

narrower, less than fifty feet now of level ground between slabs of basalt and granite that slanted
upward.

Above, a cloud skittered over the sun, blocking it
out for a moment. Spur looked up and saw a row of
thunderheads building. They could mean refreshing
rain, a thunderstorm, possibly lightning as well.

He went back to the matter at hand. There were
some slabs of rock ahead where Hoffer could be
hiding. He saw no blush of new green that might
show where a spring seeped from the ground,
though there should be a spring somewhere in there.

Spur saw a dove fly up from a perch ahead, but
there was no more activity. The bird probably had
not been flushed up by Hoffer.

Where *was* the bastard?

Spur checked the next cover, several yards up the
gentle incline of the canyon and on the left side. It
would be his emergency objective.

Hoffer was still going up the valley. Halfway to
the boulder, Spur found a twenty dollar bill, one of
the counterfeits. Spur put it in his pocket and kept
moving. The length of Hoffer's stride was shorter
now and the toes were dragging dirt with each step.

Hoffer was getting tired. How much farther could
he go?

When Spur got to the boulder, he paused. The
canyon went straight ahead for what looked like a
mile, moving up the mountain gradually and
narrowing slightly. Hoffer could be anywhere up
there. Trees dotted the sides of the canyon now, and
ahead the entire floor and sides were carpeted with
evergreens.

Spur tried to put himself in Hoffer's place. Why
had he come up here except for water and shade?
There was no good reason. It was getting hotter,

and so far no water. Hoffer might be lost, disoriented and simply going the wrong way. Possible. He might even have lost his mind.

McCoy scanned the area ahead. There was no sign of another human being. If Hoffer continued in this direction he would have a two hundred mile walk before he found a house or a settlement.

The merchant had to be out of his mind. Spur stood and found the tracks and moved forward again. He had picked out an emergency shelter twenty yards forward, but kept his glance mostly on the tracks.

The toes were digging short trails now with each step, dragging in the dirt before lifting out on every move. It was the sign of a man almost at the end of his endurance.

Far off to the west, Spur heard a roll of thunder. The storm was coming.

He concentrated on the prints. There was no walking stick or crutch or cane. Hoffer should be good for another mile before he collapsed.

The shot came as a surprise to Spur. He heard the report and almost at once a round whistled past his head. Spur dove into the dirt and rolled, came to his feet and sprinted ten yards left to his boulder for cover. One round whined off the granite upthrust and Spur ducked lower.

"McCoy, you asshole! Why don't you leave me alone?"

It was Hoffer's voice, strained, scratchy, but lucid.

"Hoffer—out for a nice little walk? Looks like you're getting tired. How about a drink from my canteen?"

Another slug slammed off the rock that protected Spur.

"I'll take your whole canteen just as soon as I ventilate your body with lead!"

"You're not much better shooting a man than you are at hanging him, Hoffer."

Three more shots hit the big boulder. Spur grinned. He wondered how many cartridges the man had.

"Come get me, you damned lawman!"

"No hurry," Spur said. "Figure to wait a while. I got water and grub, wait until you get so thirsty that you can't even spit."

Two more shots churned the air just over the top of the boulder.

Spur looked around the far side. There was more cover ten yards ahead. He could waste two shots and get that far in one rush. He watched the rocks ahead and to the right and soon saw a hat poke up, then two eyes and a sixgun.

"Gotcha!" Spur said softly. He pulled his feet under him, crouching, ready to spring forward. The hat came a little higher and Spur sent one round at it, then jolted forward and fired one more shot before he slid behind the new location and waited.

"Moved, I'd wager," Hoffer said. "Not that it matters, but you were right about prison. I did six years hard time in New York, got out, dug up fifty thousand dollars I had hidden and began passing it until I had ten thousand good dollars. Then I came West and opened up my store, or rather bought in and then married the rest of it." He laughed. "Hell, that's a better way than printing money—marry it! Of course it can be a little hard on the nerves."

"So why did you try counterfeiting again?"

"It's like a fever. I got a plate and my tools, and once I got started it's like painting a picture. You have to finish it. I'm good. One of the best alive. Always have been. I'm an artist."

"You're a killer. You shot down both your partners."

"I didn't need them anymore. Partners become a liability. Nothing personal, just business."

Spur used two more rounds as he rushed forward again. He reloaded his revolver as he lay behind a smaller boulder. He had sixteen rounds left. He had to remember that.

"I'm going to take you in, Hoffer."

"Not a chance. I'll save my last round for my own brain if it comes to that. I figured I'd get you up here away from the stage, kill you and then walk out and catch the stage no matter which way it was going. With you dead it wouldn't matter. And I'd have almost a million dollars, all my own!"

"But first you have to kill me, Hoffer." Spur stood up suddenly. "Over here, Hoffer!" he shouted, paused a moment then dropped behind the rock.

Six shots came in rapid order, over and around and into the rock, but none of them hit Spur. He checked the rounds in his belt loops again, and stared in disbelief. The ammunition was all for a .45 weapon. He had taken four from the near end and they were .44 and fit, but there was only one more .44 round. He was suddenly down to six rounds, not sixteen!

Lightning zig-zagged through the darkening sky to the west, and in seconds the rumbling thunder rolled over them.

"You're going to get wet," Spur shouted.

"*You're* going to get dead!"

Spur saw the intensity of the rain as it battered the ridge just to the west, moving toward them. A

dozen more lightning bolts stabbed the earth and
Spur looked at the sides of the canyon. Too steep to
climb, but there were a few spots where he could get
up part way. He watched the rain up the canyon and
knew it was a cloudburst. He fired one shot at
Hoffer's rock, retreated ten yards and slanted
twenty more up the side of the ravine.

The higher ground seemed like a good idea, a
damn good plan!

Hoffer tried to move, but Spur pinned him down
with another shot. (He was down to four, but Hoffer
didn't know that.) Spur made one more dash up the
slope and threw himself into the dirt behind a
boulder and a pine tree just as three shots jolted the
foot thick pine.

"Good shooting," Spur called.

A moment later the rain hit them, light at first,
then a downpour. Spur spent one more round
sending it just over Hoffer's rock. Hoffer edged over
the rock and then dropped down. Spur had to fire
again; he did, hitting the rock. Two rounds left.

Before Hoffer could try to move, Spur heard it. At
first it was a soft rumble that he thought was
thunder, then it turned harsher and a moment later
was a driving roar. He looked above, up the side of
the canyon wall. There was no other safe spot. Spur
guessed he was forty feet above the bottom of the
gully and he had a rooted tree to hang onto.

"What the hell is that thunder when there ain't no
lightning?" Hoffer screeched over the sound of the
rain.

Spur didn't tell him. Once before he had been
caught in a ravine during a thunderstorm and had
nearly drowned as he learned his lesson.

The roar became louder and as Spur looked
through the rain he could see the growing wall of

water a half mile away, racing, roaring and crashing down the water course. His only hope was that by the time it reached him, it would have spread out enough to pass below his forty foot elevation.

Spur put one more round into the soft soil behind the rock where Hoffer crouched.

One shot left.

"Like the rain, Hoffer?"

"Wet as hell. Why don't the two of us call a truce until it stops?"

"No truces and no prisoners, that's my new motto, Hoffer."

The gunman below fired three times, and a chip of bark from the pine tree tore into Spur's cheek. Blood ran down his face. He wiped it away and looked at the raging waters.

"That noise!" Hoffer shouted. "A damn flood is coming down this gully. We got to get out of here!" Hoffer ended on a scream of terror.

"You move a foot away from that rock and I'll cut you in half with six .44 slugs!" Spur bellowed. "Just give me the chance, killer!"

Hoffer edged over the rock, then dropped down. He stood up once, then dropped just as Spur sent a round through the space he had been in a fraction of a second before.

Spur checked the gun belt again. Damn! He was out of ammunition!

The roar increased; he could barely shout over it.

"Give me another chance, Hoffer. It's a nice, clean way to die!"

Hoffer snarled four rounds at Spur, then hunkered down out of sight.

Spur watched the water. He could climb maybe ten feet up the pine tree if he had to. Lower limbs had died and broken off, leaving sturdy spike-like hand and foot holds up the trunk.

The water was less than a hundred yards away.
Spur watched it and Hoffer's rock. The little man
had not moved.

The water crashed and smashed through the
bottom of the canyon. It must be moving faster
than a horse could gallop—twenty, maybe twenty-
five miles an hour! As fast as a railroad train!

Spur looked out and saw that he was almost level
with the top of the flood waters. Logs boiled and
churned in the flood, trees popping to the surface.

Below he could see large boulders roll. Then the
upper part of the water overwhelmed them as it
surged lower, seeking its level.

When the water was twenty yards away, Hoffer
must have seen it clearly.

"NOOOO!" he screeched, jumped up and fired
once at Spur, then hobbled downstream. His right
leg had been injured, and he dragged it as he tried to
run.

The water came surging almost on top of them
then, and Spur scrambled up the tree, hoping the
tree roots and rocks on the side of the canyon wall
would hold.

20

Spur watched the water surge against his tree. It was three feet below his boots. He looked down at Hoffer.

The fat little man was running now, his hurt leg forgotten as he charged down the slight incline. But the water charged faster. A surge of foamy water teased his feet and he slipped. Then the thirty-foot high thundering mountain of water billowed over him, sucking him into its center, crashing down on top of him and churning him into the middle of a vast maelstrom of angry water, plunging tree trunks, brush and limbs from the timbered slopes above.

Spur watched downstream as far as he could see, but there was no sign of Josh Hoffer.

Spur looked to the west, sunshine gleaming on the wet mountains.

The rain slackened, then misted and at last stopped.

He could see the water dropping lower and lower

below him. Five minutes later, the water was low
enough so Spur could climb back down to the base of
the pine. A slippery coating of mud clung to the
sides of the canyon. When he went down it, he would
be on a greased slide.

After another twenty minutes the sun broke
through overhead as the storm slashed on toward
the east.

It was over an hour before the water had drained
away. Now there was only a small stream in the
center of the canyon. Spur began to move down the
wall. There was no way to climb up. He lost his
footing and skidded, dropped to a sitting position
and slid down the side to a big rock that stopped
him.

He stood, wiped some of the mud off his pants and
picked his way cautiously the last twenty feet to the
bottom of the canyon.

Mud, branches and a log now and then clogged the
small valley. He made his way lower. As he went, he
watched for any sign of the body.

There was no chance that Hoffer could have sur-
vived such an onslaught. If he had lived long enough
without oxygen to get to the surface, the flotsom
and current would have torn his body apart.

Spur spent another hour moving down the gully,
watching everywhere that a body might be lodged,
but found nothing. By the time he came out of the
mouth of the canyon into the valley itself, he was
wondering if he could ever prove that Josh Hoffer
had been drowned in the flash flood. The sheriff
would be extremely interested in such proof.

Spur checked the mouth of the gully again,
crawled over a muddy pile of trees and branches,
then gave up.

He sat on a dry spot and let the sun dry the water out of his clothes.

The stage coach driver would report the shots, and he surely would see the dead man alongside the stage road. That he would report to the sheriff. When the rig came to the dead horse and the surrey, the driver would have to stop it and move the horse, or at least the brush Spur had piled up to stop the surrey. When he did that, he would find the boxes almost filled with twenty dollar bills. The passengers would go wild. So might the driver.

But if Spur knew the character of these stage coach drivers, he would gather the money and turn it over to the sheriff, which meant the sheriff should have known about the money and the dead man about two hours after the coach passed here. It would take another two hours for the sheriff and a posse to ride to the scene.

Spur stood and angled for the stage road. He would walk back to the surrey and wait for the sheriff. Hopefully the posse would bring along an extra horse. Then he could have some help in search-ing for Hoffer's body.

By the time Spur stumbled into the shade where the surrey and dead horse were, he was too tired to wonder how far he had walked. Only two or three miles, but he was dead tired. He looked down the road toward town and saw that the brush had been pulled out of the roadway, but he could see no one coming. It could be a while.

Spur stretched out in the shade and went to sleep.

The first thing Spur heard when he awoke was the cocking of a six-gun. He didn't move. A boot lowered slowly but firmly on his right hand that lay by his side.

"I got a live one over here, Sheriff!" the man over Spur called.

"Look, I . . ."

"Not another word until the sheriff gets here!" the man said with a touch of anger. "Right over here, Sheriff."

Spur could hear men moving over the ground, then a soft chuckle.

"Okay, Lon, you can ease off. He's one of the good guys."

"Huh?"

"He's not the killer we're looking for."

"Oh."

The boot moved.

"You can sit up now, McCoy, without getting your head blown off."

Spur came to a sitting position slowly and saw Sheriff Sloan holding a Henry repeating rifle.

"Looks like you took a mudbath. That before or after you shot Turner?"

"After Joshua Hoffer shot him. Way after. You get the counterfeit back?"

"From the stage?"

"Right."

"Two packages. Had to search the passengers. Found another two thousand dollars. I think we have it all."

"There's more out along the trail somewhere. Hope you can spare a man or two to help me look for it."

"Possible."

"You wouldn't have a spare horse, would you? I got a free ride in the surrey with my hands tied and a gun aimed at my midsection. Hoffer wanted to hang me again!"

"Looks like he didn't quite make it. Where *is* Hoffer? Or is that too delicate a question?"

"I want to find him as bad as you do, Sheriff. Last time I saw him a flash flood about thirty feet high was crashing down on top of him in a gully up the road."

"But it missed you. You didn't happen to hang the Jasper first, did you? Then dump him in the flood?"

"If he's got a neck left, you can check for rope burns. You found Turner. I got lucky with a boulder from the cliff and busted up his leg. Hoffer didn't want to wait for Turner, so he killed him."

"Eye witness?"

"Right."

The sheriff shifted his stance, looked at Spur, then his hand brushed past his six-gun.

"Those are two of the leading citizens of our town. Hoffer wasn't by any chance just along for the ride, was he?"

Spur grinned. "Hell no. He was the brains, the third man, the engraver, in this counterfeiting scheme. I figure that was one reason he wanted me hanged out there at the Ned Bailey place when we first met."

"And you say Hoffer is dead in the gully somewhere?"

"Probably under some brush, or hung up on a log or a rock and covered up by a foot of silt. Still wish I had the chance to hang him. He went too easy, too fast."

"Dead is dead."

Spur grunted. "You got a horse for me? I'll show you where if you want to check it out. I could also use your canteen."

An hour later five men began picking their way through the outfall of the death canyon. Hoffer was

there somewhere; all they had to do was uncover
him.

It was almost dusk when one of the horses shied
away and backed up from a pile of brush. Hoffer was
under it. The men dug him out and Sheriff Sloan
washed off his neck with water from his canteen.

"Neck is broken," the sheriff said. "But no rope
marks." He looked at Spur. "I'm glad about that.
Now let's get the rest of that money found before
dark and get things moving."

The men cleaned up the area near the surrey and
hitched one of the extra horses they had trailed in
the traces. They loaded Turner's body in and found
a dozen packets of money on the body. Spur threw
the cash in a gunny sack. Turner's carpetbag was
half full of the packets of bills. The men in the posse
looked at the cash and couldn't believe it. Spur
showed them the serial numbers—all the same, all
counterfeit.

Where the two counterfeiters had lightened their
luggage of packets of bills, the men picked up
another hundred thousand dollars' worth.

Then the real search began along both sides of the
trail as they tried to find where Hoffer had hidden
his carpetbag with the rest of the fake money.

Spur offered the man who found the bag a double
eagle gold piece. Interest picked up. Twenty dollars
was a month's wages for lots of men around Twin
Falls.

An out-of-work cowboy found the bag behind
some heavy brush fifty feet off the stage road. Spur
handed him the twenty dollar gold piece as the rest
cheered.

They had carried Hoffer's body back to the surrey
and they now loaded the merchant's remains in the
back seat and got the small party under way. They

had a mount for Spur. He talked with the sheriff, then rode out ahead with two other men and hurried back toward Twin Falls. It was almost eight o'clock when they arrived.

Spur had a long, hot bath, then the best steak in the dining room. He had just finished eating when Sheriff Sloan pulled up a chair and stared hard at him.

"You wrapped up here?"

"Not quite."

"If you're thinking about young Boots Dallman, don't. I went back over my memory, and I can't remember a single thing he did to help the lynchers. He didn't even hold their horses."

"He was too drunk to know what was going on," Spur said.

"Then why not leave him alone?"

"Boots? Wouldn't think of hurting him. Fact is, I had a nice long chat with him and his wife just a couple of days ago."

"That so? And you didn't hang him?"

"Not a chance. Seems like a solid citizen. He even swore on his mother's grave and in front of his wife that he was giving up booze and wild women."

The sheriff looked relieved. "Sounds like you scared the shit out of him."

Spur laughed. "You might say that."

"Then you are through here?"

"Not quite. You and I still have to find the engraved plates those bills were printed from."

"Hoffer's Mercantile?"

" 'Pears as how. You free for the evening?"

An hour later they were still hunting. Mrs. Hoffer watched them critically, making them put back every box they opened, and keep the store in order.

"I want to open up in the morning, and goodness knows I can't with things spread all around!"

She knew nothing of the counterfeiting though she had been married to Hoffer for three years. Her ex-husband had started the Mercantile twenty years ago and built it into a thriving business before he died in the smallpox epidemic of sixty-eight.

"I ran it before, I can run it again," she told the sheriff calmly when he informed her of Hoffer's death. She knew nothing of his former life, nothing at all.

"Where in hell would *you* hide two engraving plates?" Spur asked the sheriff.

"Somewhere no one would think to look. Like in a framed picture on the wall?"

They checked the four hanging pictures, but none contained the plates.

Mrs. Hoffer suggested the cracker barrel, but the wooden barrel did not harbor the plates.

Spur next looked at the bean bin. It was a wooden affair that held about twenty gallons and was nearly full of white navy beans.

He pushed his hand into the bin and found nothing.

Mrs. Hoffer came up clucking, "No, no! We'll take them out with a scoop into a flour sack. We keep things as clean as we can around here. Notice the covers over the beans and flour and crackers?"

She scooped and Spur held the sack. Halfway down in the bean bin, they found the plates, carefully wrapped in heavy waxed paper.

Spur took them out, broke each one in half over his knee then stared at them.

"Beautiful work," Spur said. "The man was an artist."

Mrs. Hoffer snorted. "He was also a criminal and

a murderer. You say he killed poor Mr. Wintergarden, too?"

The sheriff said Hoffer had admitted to shooting
Wintergarden. He thanked Mrs. Hoffer and Spur re-
wrapped the plates in the waxed paper.

"Now, Sheriff, I'm starting to finish my work.
Next on my agenda is a thin cheroot and a long,
peaceful night's sleep."

"The counterfeit bills—what should we do with
them?"

"Tomorrow we'll have a bonfire. We'll need witnesses. We'll burn them in a fireplace or a stove so
we can control it. Tonight, keep the boxes in one of
your cells. I have another two thousand dollars'
worth I'll donate to the fire tomorrow."

They stood there a minute remembering.

"Oh, did you tell the widow Turner about her
loss?"

"Yes, this afternoon when the stage came in. The
driver checked the body and found identification on
it. So I told her. Strange, she didn't seem very
upset. I'd guess the widow Turner will not have a
long period of mourning."

Spur thanked the sheriff and went back to his
hotel room. The door was locked. Good. He was
feeling the effects of almost no sleep the night before
and the long walk. A visitor right now would not be
welcome.

He stepped inside his door, locked it and moved to
the dresser where he struck a match and lit the
lamp.

A woman laughed softly behind him. He turned,
holding the lamp, and saw Eugenia Turner sitting
on the bed. Beside her was Sue, the girl from the
laundry. Both were bare to the waist, and Eugenia
had her arms around the younger girl.

"Well, it's about time you got back," Eugenia said sweetly. "We got tired of waiting for you, so we decided to start without you."

"Hello, Mr. McCoy," the younger girl said. "I thought it might be nice to come visiting and see if you can help me get a better job. I hope you don't mind." She stretched, and her naked breasts surged forward and danced a highland fling.

She put her hands down and cupped both her breasts. "My titties have been just waiting for you to come!"

"Isn't she a delight!" Eugenia said. "She's so young and unspoiled and eager to please. At first I resented her waiting here for you when I came in. Then we began to talk and we decided you had more than enough for both of us, and we're both understanding, so we decided to share you!"

The women stood and undressed Spur slowly, stripping off his clothes, giggling and feeling his muscles and remarking how strong he was and how well built.

Sue drew the honor of pulling down his underwear and when his penis popped out stiff and sturdy, she squealed and knelt down, took half of it in her mouth and began sucking.

"Darling, you have to take your turn," Eugenia said, pushing Sue away. They urged Spur back on the bed and then eagerly stripped off the rest of their clothes. At once each began ministering to him.

Sue hovered over him, then lowered one big breast into his mouth. Spur caught it, chewed and licked it and purred.

"I think I'm in heaven and the angels have just arrived," he said.

As he said it, Eugenia kissed the tip of his man-

hood and then took the whole shaft in her mouth.
Spur almost climaxed.

He controlled himself and soon had the tables
reversed, with the women sitting on the bed as he
sampled the four hanging tits. Sue's were large,
with a little sag from their bulk and large pink
areolas topped by blushing pink nipples that grew
and quivered when he licked them.

Spur concentrated on the younger girl a moment,
his mouth on her breasts, one hand exploring
between her legs, and she suddenly screamed. Her
whole body went rigid and she fell backwards on the
bed and jolted through the most intense climax
Spur had ever seen in a woman.

Eugenia slid back on the bed, her eyes wide, one
hand covering her mouth.

It was over in twenty seconds, and Sue sat up and
wiped sweat off her forehead.

"Damn! That was fine!" she said. "I win the prize,
I beat everybody."

They all laughed.

"What we need is some wine and cheese," Spur
said.

Eugenia pointed to two paper sacks near the door.
"That comes later," she said. "Fuck first, food
second."

The strain of the past two days seeped out of Spur
as he rolled over on Eugenia, spread her legs and
without any preliminaries, drove his tool deeply into
her.

She whimpered for a minute, then swore at him
and her hips began a pounding against him that he
had to rush to keep up with.

Sue sat naked beside them, observing them with
interest.

"Watch and learn," Sue said as the naked bodies

rocked together in perfect rhythm to the explosion that sent them both into temporary oblivion. They had both climaxed at nearly the same time.

"Hell, I'm going to see what we have to eat," Sue said then. She opened the sacks and spread the food out on the dresser top beside the lamp. There was another lamp in the closet and she got it out, lit it and put it on the wash stand.

Spur and Eugenia joined her a few minutes later.

"We have two kinds of wine, and three kinds of crackers and two kinds of cheese," Eugenia said.

Spur sampled both kinds of wine and the cheese, sitting on the room's only chair, a straight-back wooden one. Sue came over, bent for him to kiss her breasts, then pushed his legs apart and quickly brought him to erection with her mouth from where she knelt in front of him.

"My turn," she said. "Don't move. I want you right there." She edged forward, straddled his spread legs, and then positioned herself over his lance. Holding it, she lowered herself on the stiff tool.

Spur growled and she moaned softly as flesh penetrated flesh until they were joined pelvis against pelvis.

"Now *that* is wild fucking!" Sue said. She lifted up and dropped down and lifted and dropped. Each time his penis slid across her clit it brought a shriek of delight from her.

"Yes, yes! More, more!" she said. She took his hands and put them on her breasts, then gyrated and bounced until she climaxed again. This time she fell forward on Spur and he held her as she went rigid again, as spasm after spasm shook her body and left her weak and drained.

Spur lifted her off and lay her on the bed. He still

had an erection. Eugenia bent over him.

"Poor darling, you didn't get your turn." She went down on him with her mouth and gently played with his balls as she mouthed him until he couldn't stand it any more and shot his seed into her willing mouth. She swallowed time after time, and then he sank back on the bed, spent and satisfied.

Later they had more wine and cheese. Before long, the wine was gone, but Eugenia brought out two more bottles. "I wanted to be sure you have plenty," she said.

"I hope you ladies can stay all night," Spur said.

They both nodded.

"Good. Wake me up later. I need a nap." He fell on the bed and went to sleep at once.

They woke him up twice during the night, and each time they all sampled each other. By morning all three were so exhausted that they slept until noon.

Spur got up and dressed quietly. Sue looked up once but he kissed her eyes closed and she slept again.

When Spur got to the sheriff's office, he could tell they had been waiting for him. He took out the box of twenties he had brought from his room.

"I think this is the last of them, Sheriff. I suggest you save three of them and mount them in a picture frame under glass as a good example of expert forgery. You can also put one counterfeit under glass for each of the banks in town. Most of them wouldn't know a counterfeit if it had a sign on it!"

They used a woodburning heater in the back room of the office, and spent three hours burning up the fake money.

"Now you can tell your friends that you burned up a million dollars," Spur said to the deputy who helped him. He had the deputy and the sheriff sign a statement that every bill except six being held under display glass had been burned and totally destroyed.

"There probably are a few more around in circulation, Sheriff," Spur said. "Whoever has them will just have to take the loss. You might talk to Mrs. Hoffer. She might stand the loss, or you could take whatever the loss is out of the assets of the newspaper office and equipment. That press is a valuable piece of goods."

They talked a while, then Spur started back to the hotel. He was going to have to think about moving out to Pocatello and then down toward Salt Lake City. He'd wait for the stage; maybe a few days here in Idaho would get his throat healed up. He changed directions and walked to Doc Rawson's office. The medic scowled and scolded him for the rough treatment he had given the rope burn on his neck. The doctor bandaged it and told him to come back in two days.

Spur grinned. Doctor's orders! He had to stay for at least two more days. He hurried to his hotel room, wondering what new delight his two roommates might have thought up.

On the way, he bought a dozen bottles of cold beer, six kinds of cheeses, and a whole sack full of crackers. It wouldn't do to run out of food. Between the three of them, they had plenty of everything else.